D1528042

THE NEARNESS OF YOU

THE THORNTONS BOOK 1

IRIS MORLAND

WITHDRAWN

1

"James Daniels?"

"It's Flannigan," Sara Flannigan said automatically to the nurse before turning to her son James. "Time to go in."

James shrugged as he continued to play his video game, but he followed his mother into the back of the doctor's office without any more protest. Six years old and already as stubborn as any adult, Sara reflected with an inward shake of her head. James was the love of her life ever since he'd been placed in her arms, all red and wrinkly and screaming to the heavens.

"Let's get the boring stuff out of the way," the nurse said as she got James's height and weight before ushering them into one of the rooms.

Sara hated the smell of these rooms—antiseptic and cold, the paper on the tables crackling as James would inevitably fidget from boredom. They hadn't been in a doctor's office in six months, not since James's amazing pediatrician in Seattle had told her that her son was healthy, still in remission, and not in need of constant doctor's visits.

But when she'd felt his swollen lymph nodes in his neck, Sara had made an appointment for him to see a family doctor here in the small town of Fair Haven, where they had moved just two months ago. That doctor hadn't taken her concerns seriously.

So, now she was here, seeing the best pediatric oncologist in Fair Haven to make certain her son's cancer hadn't returned.

"Everything looks good. I'll let Dr. Thornton know you're here." The nurse smiled at James, who continued to play his video game, kicking his heels against the table.

Sara rubbed her hands. She should've brought a sweater. Why were doctors' offices so damn cold? She'd never been in one that didn't result in her shivering from the blast of air conditioning no matter the time of year.

She told herself that more than likely James's swollen lymph nodes were nothing. Probably just a cold. His cancer had been in remission for over four years, but she couldn't stop the memories flooding her all the same. He'd had the same symptoms when he'd been just a toddler, and she'd assumed it had been nothing. Until the doctor had told her the tumor had spread to his bones and they were lucky it hadn't spread to his bone marrow just yet...

"Mrs. Daniels," Dr. Thornton said as he entered the room.

When Sara looked up from her clenched fists, she had to keep her jaw from dropping open.

This was Dr. Thornton? This gorgeous man, barely in his thirties, with dark hair and deep green eyes?

Sara swallowed against a suddenly dry throat. "It's Flannigan," Sara replied lamely, completely tongue-tied. She hadn't had time yet to legally change back to her maiden name after her divorce; thus, she was constantly reminded that she had been married to her cheating ex once upon a time.

But her cheating ex disappeared from her thoughts as she realized that not only was her doctor one of the well-to-do Thorntons of Fair Haven, Washington, but that he didn't even have the grace to grow up to be fat and ugly, too.

Of course he was a Thornton. She'd read his last name online, but for whatever reason, she'd been so worried about James that she hadn't put two and two together. That was just her luck, wasn't it?

Of course he was beautiful. Tall and muscular, he filled out his doctor's coat too well. She'd known that his father was a doctor, but she hadn't known that the eldest Thornton had pursued medicine as well.

The entire Thornton family was considered royalty in Fair Haven. Wealthy, beautiful, and talented, their six children had always been the most popular kids in school. While Sara had grown up in a trailer park with her alcoholic mother and angry younger sister, the Thorntons had represented a life she could only imagine in her dreams. To have both parents—successful and healthy—in your life? To drive brand-new cars, attend the best schools, play any sport or take up any after-school activity you wanted without worrying about the expense? Sara had had to give up on playing in band in sixth grade when her mom could no longer make payments on the cheap rental flute she'd gotten Sara to play. She remembered the shiny new flute Lizzie Thornton had gotten that same year, and how Sara had been green with envy.

Dr. Thornton glanced up, and Sara's reverie was broken. "Flannigan. I know that name. Are you...?"

"Ruth Flannigan's daughter? Yes, that's me."

His expression changed, like he was seeing her for the first time. If she didn't know better, she'd think he was checking her out.

But he turned away, and Sara told herself she was imagining things. As if one of the snobby Thorntons would glance her way! She was all too aware of what they thought about people like her, people who had grown up poor and with an absent father and an alcoholic mother. Dr. Thornton—Harrison Thornton—had been infamous in school for driving a Porsche to school after he'd turned sixteen. Sara remembered getting off the bus at the junior high next door to the high school and seeing that bright red car pull into the school parking lot, Harrison looking like the coolest guy on the planet.

Harrison wasn't that cool young teenager anymore. Now, he was a self-assured man who exuded confidence in every move he made. Sara couldn't help but watch him with interest, telling herself she was merely intrigued. She wasn't attracted to him. She wasn't thinking about how warm his hand had been when she'd shaken it, or how he could easily be mistaken for some famous actor, with his chiseled good looks, wide shoulders, and imposing stature.

"And you must be James." Harrison held out his hand to her son, which James took after a moment's hesitation. "How are you today?"

James shrugged. This had become his favorite gesture as of late. "Fine."

"His lymph nodes are swollen," Sara interjected. "He had similar symptoms when he was first diagnosed."

Harrison nodded, sitting down. He flipped through his chart. "He was diagnosed with neuroblastoma at age twenty-two months, correct? And he's been in remission...for almost four years?"

"Yes, that's correct. When he was diagnosed, it had already spread to his left femur."

Sara could rattle off every symptom, every issue, every diagnosis related to James's cancer without blinking. She'd fought the disease with only herself to lean on, as her ex-husband had preferred to avoid all of the appointments and doctors' visits as much as he could. Sara's world had become cancer, cancer, cancer. When James had finally gone into remission, part of her hadn't known what to do with herself.

"He hasn't had any other symptoms?" Harrison scribbled some notes.

"None, although he has a large bruise on his right shin bone that concerns me."

"Mom, I told you, Travis kicked me when we were playing soccer." James continued to kick his heels against the table. "I'm *fine.*"

"You probably are fine, but it's better to be safe than sorry, right?" Harrison got up to put on some gloves before beginning his examination. "Have you felt tired at all? Sick to your stomach?"

James shook his head.

"How's school going?"

"Fine."

Sara sighed. "He started first grade this past fall. He's been placed in the gifted program." She couldn't help but be proud of that accomplishment. She'd struggled in school, but seeing her boy be at the top of his class already? Her chest swelled with satisfaction.

"Really? That's great. What do you like to do for fun?" Harrison looked in James's ears and mouth as he rattled off his usual questions.

"I play soccer. It's fun, although I get in trouble when I touch the ball with my hands."

Harrison chuckled, which made a shiver run up Sara's spine. Why did he have to be so damn attractive? It wasn't fair.

"I was never very good at soccer," he admitted. "I prefer basketball. You can touch the ball all you want in basketball."

James frowned. "Jack Talbert said I was too short to play basketball and that I'll never grow bigger than I am now."

"Well, I can tell you that Jack Talbert can't see the future, but more importantly, one of my best buds isn't very tall and he's the best point guard I've ever seen."

James's eyes widened. "Really?"

"Really. Being tall is helpful when playing basketball, but there are tons of players out there who play and aren't seven feet tall." Harrison winked. "Now, let's feel these lymph nodes of yours."

Sara held her breath as he examined her son's neck. Both nodes had seemed larger than normal when she'd checked them, like oversized rubbery bumps. James had told her they didn't hurt, which just concerned her more. When he'd been diagnosed, he'd had the same exact symptoms.

She tried to push away the wash of anxiety that filled her belly. If James's cancer came back, she'd have to quit her job to care for him. When he'd been diagnosed as a toddler, she'd been a stay-at-home mom while Kyle had worked full-time. But she'd just started working as a third-grade teacher here in Fair Haven. How would she support them both if James were sick?

Harrison sat back down to make some notes.

On the edge of her seat, Sara finally blurted, "Well?"

"Based on just the swollen lymph nodes, I'm fairly certain the cancer hasn't returned," he replied in a calm voice. "That being said, we want to be sure of these things, so I'm ordering a blood test just in case."

James let out an annoyed sigh. Sara knew he was beyond tired of needles.

"And if his cancer has returned?" she asked in a tight voice.

"Then we'll make a plan for treatment. We can do the blood test right here today, and we'll have results by the end of the week, if not sooner."

She let out a breath. Her anxiety continued to simmer in her gut, but seeing her boy playing his game and kicking his heels, she had a difficult time believing that he was sick again.

She just prayed she was right.

∽

HARRISON THORNTON WATCHED as Sara and her young son were shown to the lab downstairs for the blood drawing.

He hadn't seen Sara Flannigan since he'd been in high school. If he were honest, he hadn't thought about her since then. Her family had always been considered trashy by most of the residents of Fair Haven, and although Harrison and his siblings hadn't actively made her and her sister Megan's lives difficult, they hadn't tried to befriend them, either.

Harrison winced inwardly. Guilt swamped him, along with the feeling that he wanted to deny even more—attraction.

He'd known that she'd left Fair Haven after she'd graduated from high school, and he vaguely remembered that she'd married young. He hadn't known she had a kid, and he'd had no idea that she had returned. He wondered why she'd moved back. He did know that her sister Megan had recently opened a bakery downtown. Perhaps Sara had just wanted to be closer to her mother and sister, especially with James getting older.

Harrison had been a number of years older than her, so they'd never been in the same school building at the same time, except perhaps in elementary school. Fair Haven was small enough that it only had one elementary, junior high and high school for all of its residents. The junior high and high school even shared the same parking lot, while the elementary school was only a mile away.

For some reason, something else niggled at the back of Harrison's mind in regards to Sara Flannigan, but he couldn't think of what it was. There was something else about Sara that he'd heard, but it was so long ago that the memory slipped through his fingers.

Sara Flannigan had grown up into a beautiful young woman, though. Dark-haired, curvy, with light blue eyes, she was exactly the type of woman Harrison would ask out for a drink.

But considering she was now the mother of one of his patients? Definitely no drinks. He had played that game before, and it had ended very badly.

He finished up his notes, trying to get the image of Sara's face out of his mind. He'd dealt with countless parents as a pediatric oncologist. Half of his training wasn't dealing with the children's cancer, but how to prepare and assist the worried parents who had to watch their children suffer. And even worse were the children who didn't make it. Telling parents that their child wouldn't recover?

It was the worst part of his job, and he wouldn't wish it on anyone.

"Dr. Thornton, can I speak to you a moment?"

Sara stood in the doorway.

"James, go with the nurse to the front office so I can talk to the doctor for a few minutes," she said to her son, who followed the nurse without protest.

Sara shut the door but didn't sit down. Wringing her hands, she looked pale and worried. Harrison's heart went out to her.

"Ms. Flannigan, please sit." He ushered her to a chair. "Did the blood draw go badly?"

Her eyes widened slightly. "Oh, no. James is a trooper about that type of thing. He's gotten used to it." Her smile was sad. "When you get poked and prodded and tested starting as a toddler, I think getting blood drawn is the least of your worries as a kid. Mostly he just finds it boring when a nurse struggles to find one of his veins."

"Well, I'm glad it wasn't difficult for him." Harrison took in her expression and asked in a quiet voice, "But what about you? I know this can be just as hard on the parent as on the child."

Sara wiped at her eyes, laughing a little. "I know you said it's unlikely to have come back, but I can't stop remembering that he was just fine when he was diagnosed. When his pediatrician said it could be cancer, I laughed because it seemed so absurd." She inhaled a deep breath. "But then they said he had cancer and would have to undergo chemotherapy and radiation and..."

Harrison moved his chair closer, touching her hand. Although he'd been trained to deal with parents, for some reason, Sara's plight touched him more than it usually did. Maybe because he saw how much she adored her son; or maybe it was because he wanted to know more about her as a person. Perhaps his motives were entirely selfish.

"As soon as I receive the results, I'll contact you," he assured her. "I can't say absolutely that his cancer hasn't returned, but I'm not anxious about the results. Don't let this ruin your week. Enjoy spending time with James and seeing what a smart, healthy little boy he's growing up to be."

"You're right. I mean, I'll try my best." She sniffled. "I was doing all right in the last year. He's been healthy, but anytime there's anything that might seem like the cancer has returned, I just spiral. It's exhausting."

Harrison realized he hadn't moved his hand away from hers, but he couldn't stop himself from squeezing her fingers. When she squeezed back, he felt it in his entire body.

"Have you ever talked to anyone about suffering from PTSD?" At her shocked expression, he explained, "I know most people think PTSD is for soldiers returning from war, but you went through hell. Anyone would be affected by watching their child go through something like cancer."

Sara moved her hand away from his, gazing off into the distance. "I hadn't thought about it, but maybe I should. I can't keep doing this every time James might seem sick. What happens if he breaks a bone or something? I'll be a basket case the rest of my life." She laughed, but it was a quivery kind of laugh.

Harrison wished he could hug her. Not because she was gorgeous, and clearly devoted to her child, but because she seemed like she needed a hug. But instead of hugging, he said in a reassuring voice, "You've done a great job with him, and if, God forbid, his cancer has returned, then I will help you fight it every step of the way. You have my promise."

Her eyes shone as she looked up at him. "Thank you. Sometimes I feel like the entire world is on my shoulders. Ever since my divorce..." Realizing she was probably saying too much, she stood up and held out her hand. "Thank you again, Dr. Thornton, for all of your help."

He shook her hand, and he saw in her face the crackle of attraction between them. Her eyes widened. Staring down at her, he couldn't help but marvel at how red her lips were, or how long and dark her eyelashes were.

The door creaked open behind them.

"Mom, you done?" James poked his head in.

Sara jumped. "Oh, James, yes. I'm sorry. Dr. Thornton and I were just talking." She pulled her hand away.

Harrison nodded at James, who gave him a look that seemed to say, *I know what you were thinking about my mom and I don't like it.* But then the look disappeared, and he told himself he'd been imagining it.

"I'll be in touch, Ms. Flannigan. James, best of luck with soccer. And be sure to try some basketball when you get the chance."

James nodded before tugging on his mom's arm. "Come on, I'm starving."

"Okay, okay. Bye, Dr. Thornton. Thanks again."

As Harrison watched the pair leave, he had a feeling that he was going to see more of Sara Flannigan one way or another.

2

*S*ara smiled as she watched James ride his bike outside. Looking at him, you'd never think he'd been sick, and she had a difficult time believing that he was sick again now. Her heart contracted at the thought.

Let it be nothing. Let us have a break for once.

"Can you get this?"

Sara turned to see her mother Ruth struggling with bags of groceries. At the age of sixty, Ruth Flannigan had gone to rehab for alcoholism, and after a year of sobriety, Sara wanted to believe that it would stick this time. With brightly dyed red hair and cat-eye glasses, Ruth always made an entrance, something that Sara loved as a child and hated as a teenager.

"How much did you buy?" Sara took two bags and set them on the nearby counter. She pulled out boxes of cereal—Lucky Charms, more Lucky Charms, Captain Crunch, Cinnamon Toast Crunch—and sighed. "I told you no sugary cereals. It just makes James antsy all day."

"They were on sale! Besides, let the kid live a little. A bowl of marshmallows won't kill him."

Sara didn't feel like arguing. Not today. After Ruth had gotten out of rehab, she'd called her oldest daughter to ask her to move back to Fair Haven. The alcohol had caused her mother a number of health problems, and unable to work but with no retirement, Ruth had been desperate. Sara hadn't wanted to leave Seattle, but after her divorce, somehow it had felt right. She'd gotten her mom out of her trailer, moved all three of them into their own modest house, and Sara told herself she'd done the right thing.

Even if her mother didn't listen to her about James's diet.

"Mom, I know you mean well," she said firmly, forcing her mother to look her in the eye, "but James's health is precarious. I'm not going to let anything happen to him under my watch."

Ruth looked like she was going to argue, but she just heaved a sigh, her brightly clad shoulders rising and falling. "Oh Sara, can't you see that he's totally healthy? The cancer's gone. Let the kid get dirty and eat sugar. You and I both know how short life is."

Sara turned to start unpacking groceries. Seeing that one bag was mostly fruits and vegetables, she forced herself to calm down. "I took James to see an oncologist yesterday," she admitted.

Ruth dropped a container of sour cream, which rolled next to Sara's ankle. "You did what? Why didn't you tell me?"

"I don't know. I guess I just wanted to believe it wasn't happening?" At her mother's look, guilt swamped Sara. "I'm sorry. I should've told you. It's probably nothing. The doctor himself said as much."

"But it was enough that you thought you should take him in."

Now it was Sara's turn to look away. Although Ruth had been sober for a year, Sara still didn't fully trust her. There were too many memories of her mother passed out drunk on the couch, or calling 911 when she'd drunk too much and wouldn't wake up. There were too many stints in rehab that hadn't stuck, and missed concerts, games, and PTA meetings. Sara had practically raised her younger sister Megan.

She'd gone to counseling. She knew she had to forgive her mother—eventually.

"I know you still don't trust me," Ruth said quietly, her eyes sad. "I know it's not as simple as putting down the bottle and everything goes away. My sponsor has told me over and over again to give you time, but I wish you would've told me. You already did this once alone."

Sara bit the inside of her cheek. She *had* done this alone before. For some reason, an image of Dr. Harrison Thornton entered her vision. His kind, handsome face, his reassuring touch. Had she gravitated toward him because he told her what she'd wanted to hear, or because of something more? Something she didn't want to consider for herself?

"Mom! Mom! Travis found a huge grasshopper outside!" James came running into the kitchen, throwing open the freezer to pull out a Popsicle.

"James. It's ten in the morning," Sara remonstrated. But at Ruth's raised eyebrow, she gave in. "Fine, one Popsicle. And be sure to take one out for Travis."

"He likes purple. You should come see the grasshopper. It's *green*," James said, his eyes wide.

"Jamesy, come on, show your old grandma this huge green grasshopper. Maybe we can collect some roly-polies if we're lucky."

Sara's heart swelled as she watched her mom with James and Travis, the next-door neighbor's son who was also in James's class at school. Travis had a tendency to get muddy even if the day was dry—Sara didn't know how he managed it—and he had a perpetual cowlick, but he was a good kid. She'd much rather have to clean mud off her son than take him into the hospital for radiation. And although she'd been uncertain of Ruth's involvement in her James's life, Sara had been pleased to see her mother falling into the role naturally. If Sara felt angry that she herself hadn't gotten that side of her mother when she'd been a child, well, she'd swallow that and try to move past it.

Finishing unpacking the groceries, Sara heard her phone ring. When she saw the number, she almost didn't pick up. Her stomach cramped, and she could feel a headache coming on.

Kyle Daniels, the caller ID read.

She really should've changed that to *Asshole Ex-Husband*.

"Hello?" she answered in the calmest voice she could muster.

"Sara? I thought you weren't going to pick up." Kyle laughed, which just grated on her nerves.

She and Kyle had married young, mostly because Sara had gotten pregnant and she had nowhere else to go—no money, no job, and a baby on the way. She'd wanted to believe she and Kyle could make a life for themselves, especially after James had been born, but their already flimsy marriage quickly started to fall apart when they'd added a newborn to the mix.

"How's Fair Haven? Or are you already wanting to move back to civilization?"

She made a face at the fruit bowl sitting on the table. "Did you need something, Kyle?"

"Touchy. You know I'm just kidding around. Actually, I wanted to talk to you about James."

At the mention of their son, she instantly was on her guard. Kyle had had little interest in James since his birth, and even less when he'd been sick. But after the divorce, suddenly that had all changed. Sara knew it was only to get back at her for daring to leave him.

"Look, I know you said I'd still be able to see him, but I just don't see how that's going to work with you living two hours away. I've consulted with my lawyer, and he agrees that you're violating our custody agreement with your move."

Sara stared at the fruit bowl until the vision of the bananas and apples rippled in her vision. "In case you don't remember, I have full custody of James," she said in a slow voice, anger building inside of her chest. "So I can take him to Australia if I want to."

"And whose idea was it to give you full custody? Me. Because I thought it would be best for him to live with his mother." Kyle always said the word *mother* like you'd say the word *centipede*. "But that doesn't mean you can keep him from me. I'm not going to be kept out of his life."

At that, she lost her temper. "When have you ever been in his life? You weren't there when we were living under the same roof! You didn't see him more than five times all of last year, and you lived twenty minutes away. If you really want to see him, then drive up here and see him."

Kyle, though, didn't take the bait. Sara always knew she shouldn't get angry, because he used that against her. "Now you're getting emotional, and you know I can't talk to you when you get like that," he said in that grating voice of his. "I'll have my lawyer contact yours to discuss this in a rational manner."

"You do that. Have a great day."

She hung up, letting out a loud screech of frustration. It was so loud that Ruth popped her head inside to make sure nothing was wrong.

"Just Kyle," Sara said.

Ruth nodded in understanding. "Oh, I should've known. I'll leave you alone."

Sara stood at the kitchen window as she watched Ruth help James and Travis find bugs in the grass. Drinking that in, she forced herself to calm down, but the anger wouldn't abate. She never thought she'd hate someone as much as she hated her ex-husband. When they'd been younger, she'd been impressed with his wealth and social standing, having always believed she wasn't worthy of anyone like that. She'd been so young and stupid. When she'd discovered she was pregnant, she had told him with a

mixture of joy and hope. They could be a family—a family she'd
never had growing up.

It was only until later that Sara realized that Kyle had only
married her when his parents had discovered the pregnancy. He
hadn't planned on marrying her at all.

She let out a breath. Although she had full custody, Kyle had
enough money and connections to make her life hell if he wanted
to. She'd stupidly assumed that he'd be happy when she asked for
a divorce. He'd been cheating on her for years, and the only reason
she'd stayed was because she'd had to care for James during his
cancer treatment and had needed someone to support her. It
wasn't a romantic arrangement, but she'd thought they'd both
understood that. After James had gone into remission, she'd gone
to a community college to earn her teacher's license, knowing that
she wouldn't be able to leave Kyle if she were working a minimum
wage job.

Cue Kyle refusing to give her a divorce for over a year once
she'd earned her diploma and license. When he'd finally relented,
Sara had hoped that would be the last of his capricious whims.

She'd been naïve, as always.

"Mom! Mom! Come outside and see this bug!" James ran into
the kitchen and tugged on her arm. "Grandma says it's a bee but I
think she's wrong."

Sara let herself be dragged outside, where she was promptly
shown the giant bug (not a bee, but a hornet, which caused a few
screams). She helped James collect roly-polies from off the driveway. Travis went home to get his butterfly net, although Sara
hadn't seen any butterflies around lately. Realizing the lack of suit-
able butterfly prey, Travis turned his attention to capturing slow-
moving ladybugs in his giant net.

"Were you talking to Dad?" James asked her. She'd gotten out
the sidewalk chalk, and James drew a giant peach-colored circle
next to her.

"Yeah, I was. How did you know?"

He began filling in the circle. "Because you always make that face after you talk to him. Like you've just seen a big bug in the kitchen."

She laughed, but it was a little sad. "Do I? Then I'll try not to do that anymore."

"Do you think Dad likes me?" He looked up at her.

Her heart fractured at the question. She tried very hard not to make that big-bug-in-the-kitchen face, but she probably failed. *Screw Kyle and his huge ego.*

"Of course he does," she soothed. "He's just busy, and now we don't live as close, so it's harder for him to see us."

"Then why doesn't he come here?"

Because we could live right next-door and he wouldn't care.

"He has a job, honey. You know that."

James began drawing green lines around the peach circle, his mouth creased in a frown.

If I could wish the worst things on anyone, it would be on my ex-husband.

AFTER RECEIVING James Flannigan's results back, Harrison had taken the first opportunity to call Sara himself. Normally one of his nurses would do this, but he wanted to do it himself. He told himself it wasn't because he wanted to hear her voice again.

"Hello?" Sara answered on the first ring.

"Ms. Flannigan, hello. Is this a good time?"

"Not to be rude, but is there ever a good time to hear results like this from a doctor?" He could hear the wryness in her tone.

"Good point. Well, I won't waste time. The cancer has not returned. James is in the clear."

He heard her inhale a deep breath. After he'd gotten the blood test results back, he'd been beyond relieved that the cancer had stayed away. He couldn't imagine how stressed Sara would be if she'd heard the opposite. Harrison had had too many phone calls of a different sort with parents to know that they were difficult for all parties involved.

"Oh thank God. Oh God, thank you. Thank you so much." She took another deep breath. "I needed something good to happen today. You're my hero. I feel like I should send you a gift basket."

He chuckled. "I didn't do anything. Send a gift basket to James's good health and your dedication to keeping him healthy."

"Maybe I will. Thank you again."

"I do want to check in on him in about a month. The enlarged lymph nodes do concern me. It's more of a precaution at this point, however."

"Okay, yes, of course. I'll schedule that right away."

Harrison hung up the phone after saying goodbye. It was the end of the day, and he didn't have any more patients to see. Normally he'd text his younger brother Caleb—a local police officer—and their mutual friend Heath DiMarco, but Harrison didn't feel like bar-hopping tonight. If he were honest, he'd only dated a handful of women since finishing his residency a few years ago and beginning his own practice.

But going home to his empty house sounded even worse. Texting Caleb and Heath, they agreed to meet up at the local bar, The Fainting Goat, which had the best beer in town. Fair Haven was known for two things: its gorgeous scenery and its local breweries. The latter was what kept most people around.

When Harrison entered the bar, both Caleb and Heath were already there. Caleb gave him the usual shoulder-slapping hug. With his dark hair and good looks, Caleb was popular with the ladies and had probably dated more of them than any other guy in town. It helped that he wore a police uniform most days. As a local cop, Caleb knew just about everyone's business. He was a bit taller than Harrison, which he'd rubbed in his older brother's face when they'd been teenagers, although Harrison was stockier compared to Caleb's almost lanky frame.

Heath DiMarco was the opposite of Caleb in every way: a fifth grade teacher, he wore glasses and didn't date around, although Harrison knew that his friend wasn't as awkward with the ladies as he seemed to want people to think. Heath was a handsome guy, underneath the suit jackets and messy, auburn-colored hair.

"How's it going?" Caleb asked as Harrison sat down next to him. Caleb motioned to the bartender. She gave him a heated look before sashaying over to them.

Harrison almost opened his mouth about Sara Flannigan, but he bit his tongue just in time. He couldn't breach patient confidentiality like that, and besides, if he let on at all that he was interested in her, Caleb would start grilling him.

Then again, Caleb would also know any details about her if Harrison so much as hinted an interest. So, he kept his mouth shut.

"All work, no play," Harrison said as he took his beer from the bartender. The woman gave him a look that also said she'd be willing to take on more than one Thornton man that night. Harrison ignored her. "Anything new with you, Heath?"

Heath sipped his beer. "You mean besides some of my kids deciding to set a trash can on fire and being surprised when they got detention? Not particularly." He smiled wryly. "Remind me why I went into teaching?"

"No idea. Sounds horrible." Caleb drummed his fingers against the worn countertop, like he could never stop moving. It was a tick of his brother's that Harrison had always found rather amusing, although when they'd been younger, he'd wished his brother could just sit still for more than five seconds.

"I actually didn't see the fire," Heath added, "but Ms. Flannigan did."

Harrison's attention was instantly on alert. How could he have forgotten? Sara Flannigan worked at the elementary school with Heath.

"I'm still surprised that Sara Flannigan came back here," Caleb said with a shrug. "She always seemed like she'd never come back. Can't say that I blame her."

"Why do you think she came back?" Harrison ventured.

"I think with her sister in town and her mother needing help, she wanted to come back." Heath took another sip of his beer. "Or at least that's what she hinted to me when she mentioned it."

For the stupidest reason, Harrison's gut clenched with jealousy at Heath talking to Sara about this. Was Heath interested in her? He'd be blind and stupid not to be. With her pretty face and intelligence and dedication to her son, any man would be lucky to have her.

"Her ex was a piece of work. You guys remember Kyle Daniels? He was a piece of shit." Caleb shook his head. "I pulled him over for a DUI when they were visiting a few years back, but he managed to get out of serving any time. I'll never forget how he whined about how his family would hear of this, and then he puked on my boots."

"Actually, I'm surprised you don't know Sara. Her son had cancer when he was little," Heath said. "She obviously doesn't talk about it much, but it's kind of one of those things everybody knows about, I guess."

"Yeah, I knew that." Harrison sipped his beer. *I also know that she adores her son, has a beautiful smile, and is a woman I need to stay away from, because dating patients' mothers is never a good idea.*

"You think she's over her divorce? Because I saw her at the grocery store yesterday, and damn, she's beautiful. I never remembered her being that beautiful back in school." Caleb considered. "You think she'd get a drink with me?"

Harrison gritted his teeth while Heath laughed. "Has any woman turned you down?" Heath asked.

Caleb smiled. "Not yet."

"Leave her alone. She's got a kid." Harrison knew he sounded like an ass, but he didn't care. The last thing he needed was his horn-dog brother to try to get into Sara Flannigan's pants.

Caleb raised both eyebrows. "Whoa there. What's with the grizzly bear act?" He narrowed his eyes before letting out a laugh. "Wait, is my older brother, famous bachelor, actually *interested* in a woman for once? Beyond taking her home for one night and then promptly forgetting about her?"

Harrison gave him the bird. "You're confusing yourself with me, little brother."

"Nah, I'm pretty sure that's how you roll most days. Huh, this is interesting. I'd ask if her son was a patient of yours, but I won't bother. I can see it's true on your face. Well, what the hell are you waiting for? Ask her out, otherwise I will."

Harrison rolled his eyes. "It's not that simple. Besides, I don't date women who may or may not be related to one of my patients."

Heath nodded. "I don't date any mothers, either. PTA meetings are painful enough, let alone when you're with a mom who you just broke up with."

"Good thing I rarely arrest any pretty women," Caleb said.

"Except for one," Harrison couldn't help but say slyly, wanting to get himself out of the hot seat. "You see Megan Flannigan lately? You always seemed to like Sara's sister."

Caleb grunted. "Her *sister*. If only she'd stayed far, far away from Fair Haven. That woman is a menace."

"What do you have against the sister?" Heath asked, amused.

"You remember Megan Flannigan? No? Wait, you wouldn't. Well, I arrested her the first week I started as a cop, and she's never forgiven me for it. Every time I go to her bakery I'm afraid she's poisoned my donut."

Heath laughed out loud. "Then why keep going back? But I guess if the woman is beautiful enough you'll just about take any kind of abuse."

"Fuck off. I'd sooner date a cobra," Caleb muttered. But his expression seemed to speak differently.

Harrison had a feeling his brother was more interested in Megan Flannigan than he'd care to admit, which he could understand all too well. His interest in Sara was only getting worse with each passing day.

And really, why didn't he ask her out? It wasn't the most ideal circumstance given their connection, but they certainly wouldn't be breaking any rules. Besides, given James's current bill of health, more than likely he wouldn't remain a patient of Harrison's for much longer. Then he really didn't have any excuse not to ask out Sara Flannigan.

Harrison liked women, in a general sense. He liked how they smelled, how they laughed, how they felt underneath him. He'd dated a variety of women since he'd been a teenager, and he'd had a few long-term girlfriends. Medical school had distracted him enough that he hadn't dated seriously in a long time, and then he'd done his residency in Indiana before returning to Fair Haven, which hadn't helped. Did he just need to get laid? Was that why he was so interested in Sara?

"What the hell are you assholes doing in my bar?" Trent Younger, the owner of The Fainting Goat and a number of other restaurants in Fair Haven, came up to the trio with a grin on his face. Trent went way back with the Thorntons, as he and Lizzie Thornton had dated until they'd broken up unexpectedly when they'd barely graduated high school.

Trent was tall and muscular, with bright blue eyes that Harrison had heard his sister Lizzie admit were beyond beautiful.

Lizzie had run off to be a musician and hadn't been in Fair Haven for a while now, but Trent had stayed. And, Harrison had a feeling, had been waiting for his sister to return.

"Oh, are your best customers not allowed in here anymore?" Caleb said as he gave Trent another shoulder slap like he'd given Harrison.

"I guess you guys do keep me in business. Who else will drink my shittiest, overpriced beer?"

"You probably shouldn't tell your customers they're drinking shitty beer," Heath pointed out as he sipped the beer in question.

"You guys don't count. Now, tell me something interesting because if I have to listen to my CFO talk about financial projections anymore I'm going to kill myself."

The four men moved to a table to shoot the shit, ordering more beers. As a gesture of goodwill, Trent put the second round on the house.

"Oh hey, I got a call from Lizzie," Caleb said. Harrison saw Trent visibly stiffen, but it was a tiny thing. No one else seemed to notice. "She said she might visit for Thanksgiving."

"Hasn't she been saying that for three years?" Harrison asked.

Caleb shrugged. "Yeah, but she sounded like she meant it."

Trent finished off the rest of his beer in one swig before setting down the glass. "I need to get back to work. You guys take it easy."

The trio watched the bar owner depart. Heath raised an eyebrow. "You think?"

"Yeah," Caleb drawled.

Harrison just nodded. If they could agree on anything, they were all idiots when it came to women.

3

*J*ames pressed his nose against the glass casing despite Sara telling him not to do that exact thing only five seconds earlier.

"I want a muffin! No, a donut!" He peered inside like the secrets of the world were inside.

"Hey buddy, how about you have one small donut and one small muffin?" Megan, Sara's sister, asked with a smile.

Megan had opened this bakery a year ago. Named The Rise and Shine, it served baked goods made in-house along with coffee and tea. Megan had always loved to bake when they'd been kids, and Sara had encouraged her to pursue her dream for a long time. The bakery had become a roaring success.

"Okay!" James bounced on his feet, and Sara shook her head.

"I'll take a piece of the chocolate cake and a cup of coffee," Sara said.

After getting their orders, Sara and James sat down at a table near the front. The Rise and Shine was located in the small down-town area of Fair Haven, and on this Saturday afternoon, a week after she and James had met with Dr. Thornton, they watched the populace walk down the street. Well, Sara did. James was too concerned with each of his various baked goods.

"So how's it going?" Megan pulled up a chair to sit across from them. With her red hair and bright blue eyes, she'd always been the more striking of the Flannigan sisters. She was only a year younger than Sara, but Sara had always acted like a parent of sorts for her sister when they'd been growing up. With Ruth's struggle with alcoholism, it had been up to Sara to keep food in the fridge and the house somewhat clean. The fact that they managed to stay out of foster care was a miracle—or a tragedy, depending on how you looked at it.

Sara sipped her coffee. "Mom said you're welcome to come over for dinner tonight."

At that statement, Megan made a face. Despite living in the same town, she had had little contact with Ruth over the past four years beyond coming around for various holidays. Sara knew she was still angry at their mother for their childhoods, although Sara wished Megan would at least attempt to mend fences now that their mom was sober. Sara moving in with Ruth had helped ease their relationship to some degree, but not by much.

"I'm good," Megan replied in a clipped voice. "But how are you? You guys doing okay?"

Sara had already told her sister that James's cancer hadn't returned, but she'd yet to mention that his doctor was none other than Harrison Thornton. Megan had a chip on her shoulder the size of Argentina in regards to the entire Thornton family. Sara had thought it wise not to mention the association.

But fate had other plans.

"Hey, Aunt Megan, did you know my doctor plays basketball?" James said, mouth full of muffin.

"Don't eat with your mouth full," Sara remonstrated. At Megan's questioning look, she sighed. "His doctor is Harrison Thornton."

Megan's eyes widened. "What? Are you serious? Sara, come on, you know they're the *worst*. How did you even get into his office? I thought they'd kick out anyone not up to their snobby standards."

"He's not like that. He was great with James. Besides, what happened when we were in high school is ancient history."

Megan curled her lip. "It wasn't that long ago that the Thorntons made our lives hell while spreading rumors about *you*—"

Sara held up a hand. She didn't want James repeating what Megan was saying.

Under her breath, she replied, "Like I said, that was a long time ago. I'm not going to hold it against Harrison anyway, since he had already graduated by the time I was in high school and all of that happened."

"Harrison? You guys are on a first-name basis now?"

Uh oh. Sara looked away. She prayed she wasn't blushing. "He's James's oncologist. That's it."

"And yet you're defending him and blushing like a teenager just mentioning his name. I mean, I can't blame you: I've seen him. He's handsome, intelligent, rich—"

Sara held up a finger. "Bite your tongue."

"I'm just saying, I get it. Kind of. I'll never like them, though, and don't expect me to act like they're God's gift to mankind like everyone else in this town."

"You're just bitter because Caleb arrested you."

When Megan's face turned bright red, Sara instantly regretted her words. Megan was still touchy about this particular subject and tended to shut down when it was mentioned. At the age of seventeen, Megan had been arrested for public intoxication. Officer Caleb Thornton had caught her and booked her, for which Megan had never forgiven him.

Sara rather thought it was unfair to blame Caleb for doing his job, but the one time she'd hinted as much, Megan had almost bitten her head off. She had a feeling something else had happened during the arrest that had caused Megan's particular hatred for Caleb Thornton.

James was now looking at the two women with wide eyes.

"Look, I'm sorry. Let's talk about something else." Sara finished off her coffee. "James here can recite all fifty states in alphabetical order."

James nodded. "I did it in front of the whole school yesterday."

"I don't think even I could do that." Megan smiled as she ruffled her nephew's dark hair. "You're going to be smarter than all of us."

He shrugged. "I know."

The peace was short-lived, however. Some fifteen minutes later, the two eldest Thornton brothers stepped into the Rise and Shine. Megan stiffened, while Sara looked anywhere but at Harrison because she was afraid of how obvious she'd look otherwise.

Be cool. He's James's doctor.

"Hey Megs, can you take over for a second? I need to make a call." Megan's employee Daria called from the register.

Megan made a face—not because she'd have to run her business, but because she'd have to serve the Thornton men. Sara had to bite her cheek from laughing.

"Don't you dare leave," Megan warned her before going to the register.

"Hello Ms. Flannigan, how's your day going?" Caleb Thornton leaned against the glass case. Dressed in civilian clothes, he was just as handsome as when he wore his police uniform. But Sara only had eyes for Harrison: dressed in a blue button-up with jeans, he looked casual and yummy. She couldn't help but stare at the dark hair curling right above his collar. She realized he hadn't noticed her yet. Or he was just ignoring her, which was a depressing thought.

"It's going just fine," Megan replied in a cool tone. "What can I get you two?"

"Well, if you can believe it, my brother has never been here before. So we wanted to know what you'd recommend for first-timers." Caleb grinned.

Sara couldn't help but notice her sister's face flushing. *There's definitely more to her relationship with him than pure hatred*, she thought to herself.

"It's all good, although I'm particularly fond of the pecan pie," Megan replied.

Caleb asked, "Did you make it?"

"I did."

"Then we'll get a piece for the both of us."

Harrison rolled his eyes. "I can order for myself." He turned to Megan with a charming smile that made Sara's heart pound and her stomach clench in envy. "One piece of pecan pie and your largest cup of coffee."

Megan rang them up, handing them both two steaming cups of coffee. When Harrison turned, his eyebrows rose when he noticed Sara.

She waved, and then instantly felt stupid for waving.

"Dr. Thornton!" James scrambled down from his seat. "What are you doing here?"

"Getting something to eat. How about you?"

"I just ate a muffin *and* a donut."

"Impressive." At Caleb's look, Harrison motioned at his brother. "James, this is my younger brother Caleb. He's a police officer."

Caleb held out his hand, which James took with wide eyes. "You got a gun?" he asked in awe.

Caleb winked. "Not right now. But I do have a car with a really loud siren."

James made his way back to Sara. "Did you hear that, Mom? He has a gun!"

"That's great, honey."

"Mind if I sit?" Harrison took what was Megan's chair, setting his coffee and pie down in front of him. Sara saw over his shoulder that Caleb had returned to the register to talk to Megan. Based on his grin and her annoyed face, he was needling her as much as humanly possible.

"Oh of course. Go right ahead."

Harrison smiled, which made Sara's bones melt. He didn't have a right to be this handsome! With his good looks, charm, and intelligence, he could get any woman he wanted.

So why was he sitting with Sara Flannigan, once known as the quintessential trailer trash of Fair Haven?

She resisted the urge to sink into her seat.

"How have you been?" Harrison asked as he cut into his pie.

"I recited all fifty states in front of the entire school," James interjected. "Ooh, what kind of pie is that?"

"Pecan. You want a bite?"

Harrison shared his fork and after getting a hefty bite on it, handed it to James. James smiled as he chewed.

"Good?" Harrison asked.

"Yeah. I should've gotten that instead of the donut," said James, around a mouthful of pie.

Harrison chuckled. After James had swallowed, Sara said, "What do you say?"

"Thank you."

"You're welcome." Harrison looked like he wanted to say something else, but at his glance at James, he stopped himself.

Sara's heart pounded. "Hey James, why don't you go help your aunt Megan. You can help her serve customers."

James made a face, but knowing he wasn't going to get out of this, he got down from his chair and went to his aunt. Megan looked like she could use the intervention, given that Caleb was still grilling her and making her madder than a wet hen, by the looks of things. Hopefully a six year old would keep them from coming to blows.

"They look like they're going to kill each other," Harrison remarked.

Sara nodded. "My sister is going to get herself arrested again if she's not careful." Realizing what she just said, she covered her mouth, but Harrison just laughed. "Oh geez, don't tell her I said that. She's really embarrassed about what happened."

He nodded. "Of course. Your secret is safe with me." Grinning, he bit into his pie.

Her heart warmed. If only he weren't a Thornton. If only he weren't her son's doctor. If only she weren't Sara Flannigan.

If only.

"I wanted to thank you again, for everything," she said into the silence. "I'm sure you've worked with way too many overly anxious parents."

He finished the last bite of his pie. "Not overly anxious, just concerned for very valid reasons. You aren't the first, and you won't be the last, parent who is afraid of a child's illness coming back."

She appreciated those words. Sometimes the doctors back in Seattle had made her seem hyperbolic, like she cared too much about her own son's health. When she'd questioned them on their every move, they'd given her looks that screamed, *What do you know?* But she wasn't going to let anyone do anything to her son without her understanding what it was first.

"After James went into remission, I had the stupidest thought. I wondered what I was going to do with myself now. I'd become so obsessed with his treatment that the thought of not going to the hospital, calling doctors, fighting with insurance, trying to keep him happy and comfortable as much as possible...it was like a part of me was going away." She rubbed the back of her neck. "Weird, right?"

"Sara," Harrison said in a low voice, which sent a shiver down her spine. "You're not weird. You're like any parent whose life is put on hold when their kid is sick. I'd rather deal with a hundred parents like you than one who checks out, who decides it's not worth the effort."

She knew all too well of parents like that. Kyle had already been emotionally uninvolved, but when James had been diagnosed, that had been the catalyst for him to completely disengage.

"And it wasn't that you wanted him to stay sick. You'd become so entrenched in the war, so to speak, that when it ended, it was like you had to start over." He pressed her hand. "Don't beat yourself up about fighting for your son."

She gazed up at him, and the craziest thought crossed her mind: *I could fall in love with you.*

As if realizing they were holding hands in public, they both broke contact at the same time.

Sara blushed and looked away.

∼

WHEN CALEB HAD WANTED to stop by The Rise and Shine, Harrison hadn't planned on doing anything except get a cup of coffee and something to eat. But when he'd seen Sara Flannigan sitting at a table with James, he hadn't been able to resist talking to her, especially when James had acknowledged him right away. Normally, he wouldn't approach any patient in public, but this was different. Sara was different.

He knew Caleb would grill him later about this. Caleb liked nothing more than finding out about everyone's business. He'd been accused of acting like some gossipy old woman more than once, but Caleb had just shrugged. *It's not my fault you guys think you can keep anything from me,* he'd say.

Now, sitting across from Sara, Harrison could make out both the creaminess of her skin and the dark circles underneath her eyes. But most of all, he admired how hard she'd fought—and continued to fight—for her son.

He hadn't planned on asking her out, despite Caleb's prodding. He was her son's doctor, and it was a dicey situation.

But that excuse was slowly melting away. What would a drink hurt? It wasn't a marriage proposal. He didn't give a single solitary fuck that his parents would disapprove, especially his mom, who had always disliked the Flannigans.

So he did what he always did: he took control of the situation.

"Go out with me tonight," he said quietly.

She turned and her eyes widened. "What?"

"Go out with me, for a drink."

She hesitated and looked over his shoulder at James. "I'm not sure if I can..."

"Ask your sister. Wait, don't you live with your mom? Can she watch him?"

Sara's eyes darted across his face, like she wasn't sure if he was being sincere. "Yeah, my mom can watch him," she finally admitted.

Harrison wasn't sure if she just wanted to say no and couldn't, or if there were other reasons at play here.

"Come on, one drink. That's it. If you hate it, you can leave, or I can drive you home and we won't mention it again." He smiled cajolingly.

She inhaled a deep breath. "Okay. Sure. One drink."

"Good. What's your phone number? I'll pick you up."

She seemed to want to balk at that, but he wasn't going to let her get out of this that easily. He knew she felt the attraction between them. He had a feeling her hesitation didn't lie with *him*, but with various circumstances.

After she gave him her number and he gave her his, Caleb walked up to their table, a scowl on his face.

"Anyone ever tell you your sister is a menace to society?"

Sara bit back a laugh. "What did she do now? Poison your coffee?"

"Honestly, that wouldn't surprise me."

"Come on, bro, have you really lost your touch with women?" Harrison teased his brother. "Is there one who's actually not interested in you?"

"Ha ha, you're hilarious. You're also assuming I'd be interested in *her*. Like I've said before, I'd rather date a cobra." Caleb nodded at Sara. "No offense, and all."

"Oh, none taken. My sister feels the exact same about you."

Caleb grunted right as James hurried back to their table. "Aunt Megan said that men are the worst and that she hopes they all fall off a cliff!"

"That's nice, honey," Sara responded as the men chuckled.

After they'd all finished eating, Harrison left with Sara and James, with James running ahead with to the car. Harrison leaned down to say in her ear, "Seven o'clock work for you?"

"Yes, that works. James will be in bed by then." She turned, and he couldn't help but enjoy looking at her pretty face. She had an innocence that he found beyond attractive. Although perhaps it wasn't an innocence; perhaps it was more that she could still find good in the world despite everything she'd been through. "If you drive, what happens if I want to leave early?" she countered.

He smiled, but he knew it was wolfish. "You won't, Sara. I'll have to beg you to go home by the time we're done."

"Oh really?" She smiled. "You're so sure of yourself. Has any woman turned you—or your brother—down before?"

"Not that I know of."

She rolled her eyes. "Help me to deal with any of you Thornton men. Somebody should knock you from your pedestal." But she just smiled again. "I'll see you later tonight," she said as she got in her car after he opened the door for her.

Harrison nodded. "Tonight, then."

Caleb walked up to him as Sara drove away. He could feel his younger brother's gaze on him.

"So I guess you finally asked her out?"

Harrison looked at him. "How could you tell?"

"Considering you look like you just won the lottery...be careful, though."

"I won't hurt her."

Caleb shook his head. "I'm not talking about her." When Harrison just looked at him, Caleb shrugged. "The Flannigan women are ticking time bombs."

Harrison wanted to tell him that he was just projecting his own issues with Megan onto him, but he refrained. He didn't feel like getting a lecture from his younger brother.

As he drove home, though, he couldn't help but feel that it might be a good idea to listen to his younger brother for once.

4

"You're seriously going to do this? Go on a date with Harrison Thornton?"

Sara gazed at her sister in the mirror. Megan had a look on her face that was equal parts disgust and incredulity, which wasn't helping Sara's nerves one bit.

Why *had* she agreed to go on a date with Harrison? She was a Flannigan, and he was a Thornton. Talk about two completely different kinds of people.

"Do you think I should cancel?" Sara asked.

Megan pursed her lips. "What do you want to do?"

Sara almost screamed in frustration. She didn't know! Half of her wanted to see Harrison again, while the other half wanted to run away like a scared rabbit.

She couldn't stop thinking about his smile, about how handsome and intelligent he was. How he entered a room and everyone paid attention. How he'd paid attention to *her*.

"I don't want to cancel," she finally replied. She smoothed her silky blouse down with trembling hands. "It's just a date," she repeated. She didn't know if she were saying it for her own benefit or for Megan's.

"True, and you get a free meal out of it. No way will he let you try to pay for it." Megan tugged Sara into a nearby chair. "Let me do your hair for you. The best thing you can do is be as hot as possible, and then dump him when he gets too close."

Sara rolled her eyes. "That's what you would do, not me. And we both know you're not talking about Harrison this time."

Megan shrugged, but Sara could see the strain in her sister's expression. Megan refused to talk about her hostility toward Caleb Thornton, but everyone in the entire town knew how they hated each other. Sara had a distinct feeling there was more to it than sheer hatred, though. And wasn't hatred the closest emotion to love in the human psyche? Both inspired intense reactions.

Megan began to put Sara's hair in some kind of braided up-do that Sara would never be able to replicate. After she'd told Megan about her date, her sister had at first refused to help her get ready at all. She hated the Thorntons, and she reminded Sara more than once that it was Harrison's friends who'd started rumors about her back in high school. Rumors that had caused her untold misery and made her run away from Fair Haven as soon as she'd gotten her diploma.

Sara had countered that Megan had no proof that Harrison had been involved in those rumors, so blaming him for them was ridiculous. Besides, he'd already graduated by the time Sara had started high school, so really, how could he have known while away at college? Megan had simply replied that he could've put a stop to them if he'd wanted to, and it wasn't like he hadn't returned to Fair Haven to see friends on break. He—and his entire family—ran the town. Whatever they said was law.

Tonight, Ruth had taken James out while Sara got ready. Ruth hadn't commented on Sara's date choice, but she had given her a look that had said *don't do anything stupid.*

Why did everyone think Sara didn't know what she was getting into?

"There, how about that?" Megan added one last bobby pin to Sara's hair. "Very pretty. He's not going to know what hit him."

Sara gazed into the mirror and, for the first time in a long time, she felt pretty. And young. Ever since James's cancer and her subsequent divorce, she hadn't had time to do anything but survive.

Tonight, she would have fun. No matter how her family felt about her particular date.

As the time drew nearer for Harrison to pick her up, though, her nerves only increased. Was she making a huge mistake? He was her son's doctor. If they didn't work out, she'd have to find a new one, or worse, continue to see him despite their past association. How awkward! Her palms got sweaty, and she considered turning on the AC despite the cool weather outside. It didn't help that Megan kept looking at her like she was waiting for Sara to change her mind.

She wasn't Megan. She didn't hate the Thorntons for what was, in her mind, ancient history. Although remembering the humiliation of returning to high school that morning, all those years ago, and having people whisper behind their locker doors as she walked down the hallway. *She's a slut. I heard she slept with the entire football team.* The slurs had followed her from class to class, like a trail of shadows. By the time Sara had gotten to World History last period, she'd sat down amidst a crowd of her fellow students giggling at her. Someone had poked her in the shoulder, and she'd turned to see Devin Yates grinning cruelly.

"Hey, I heard you needed some of these," he'd said as he'd tossed a string of condom packets onto her desk. The class had erupted into laughter that had only stopped when the teacher had entered. By that point, Sara had stashed the condoms away and had run from the classroom to the nurse's office.

She forced the memories away. Harrison had been at college when that had happened. It didn't make sense to blame him.

The doorbell rang. Megan got up, but Sara glared at her to sit down. She wasn't going to have her sister scare away her date.

Maybe I should tell him I can't do this, Sara thought wildly. But when she opened the door and saw Harrison standing there, wearing a striped dress shirt and perfectly tailored trousers, his hair tousled just so, all thoughts of canceling evaporated.

"Sara," he said in an appreciative tone. He took in her outfit—blouse, floral A-line skirt, and delicate heels. "You look beautiful."

She couldn't help it: she blushed. She'd laugh at herself if she could, acting like some love-struck teenager. Wasn't she a formerly married woman with a son? But all of that went out the window when she looked at Harrison Thornton.

Megan took the chance to come up behind Sara, and Sara saw Harrison's expression change.

"Megan, nice to see you," he said in a smooth voice.

Before Megan could say anything snotty, Sara took her arm and pinched her. Megan let out a yelp, but at Sara's look, she bit her tongue.

"You guys have fun. Talk to you later, sis." Megan hugged Sara before nodding at Harrison.

On the drive to the restaurant, Sara struggled with what to say. But Harrison broke the silence when he said, "Your sister is something."

Sara couldn't help it: she laughed. "That's one way to put it. She's always been like that. Her mouth got her into trouble when we were kids, and not much has changed."

Harrison smiled at her. "You were the good, responsible child, I take it? While she was the wild child?"

She swallowed against a dry throat. *Until everyone thought I was a slut, yes,* she almost responded. She bit back the words. "Something like that. I basically raised Megan, although we're only a year apart."

"I'm sorry," he said simply.

When she caught his gaze, she knew he meant it. Most people didn't think of the implications when Sara said that she raised her own sister, but Harrison's expression conveyed sympathy. But not pity.

Her heart warmed.

By the time they arrived at the restaurant, Sara's nervousness had faded away. Harrison took her to The Fainting Goat for happy hour, and they were seated at a booth near the back that provided them with some measure of privacy. She couldn't help but wonder if people were looking at them—or more correctly, wondering what a Thornton was doing with a Flannigan.

Who cares what they think? she told herself. *I'm not going to let anyone else ruin this evening.* She squared her shoulders and sat down across from Harrison, determined to have a good time. No matter what her sister, the town, or God himself said about this date.

"Did I tell you that you look beautiful?" he said after they had ordered. His gaze traced her body, and she shivered underneath the heat in his eyes. "Purple suits you. You should always wear purple."

"Even purple pants? Purple shoes? Purple hats?" she teased. "How far should this purple thing go?"

"All purple, all the time." He leaned toward her to growl, "And most especially, purple lingerie."

Her heart pounded, thinking about wearing lingerie as Harrison looked at her. Touched her. Kissed her. Normally a man saying something like that to her would've resulted in a glass of water in the face, but he said it with such easy confidence that it only made her desire him more.

God, she was in deep.

"Purple lingerie? I'll have to look into it." She traced the condensation on her glass of cider in a slow movement.

His expression darkened. She was about to ask him if he'd like to help her pick out a set when their food arrived.

"You guys need anything else?" the waitress asked.

"No, we're fine. Thank you," Harrison replied.

The waitress smiled, her blond ponytail bouncing as she walked back to the kitchen.

GENERALLY HARRISON FOUND that dates went two ways: either there was no chemistry and it ended without pursuing anything further, or there was chemistry and they went another date, then maybe another, before ending up in bed together. Rarely did any date stray from those two results.

Tonight was the exception. It wasn't that there was no chemistry—there was an overabundance of chemistry. So much chemistry that he was surprised the table wasn't vibrating from the electricity sparking between him and Sara. She kept looking up at him through her eyelashes, smiling a mysterious smile that sent him into a tailspin. Had he ever found a woman eating a salad erotic? Well, tonight he was discovering that watching Sara do just that was causing him to be crazed with need.

And they hadn't even kissed.

Maybe it was the way her cheeks flushed when he complimented her, or the way her breasts pushed against the buttons of her blouse. Maybe it was how her slim fingers held her glass of cider, or even worse, how they traced patterns on the glass itself—patterns that Harrison wanted to feel on his skin.

He wanted her. He wanted her badly. If this night didn't end with him at least kissing her, he'd probably explode from unabated lust.

"How's James? Has he been practicing any basketball lately?" he asked.

Sara smiled that warm smile she had solely for her son. "He's only asked me about twenty times when he can sign up for basketball, conveniently forgetting that I've told him that the season doesn't start until later this year. But yes, he's doing great. I can't tell you again how much I appreciate your taking my concerns seriously. I've had other physicians who tended to think I was hysterical."

She said the words with a shrug, but they made Harrison clench his fist underneath the table. What asshole had waved away her legitimate concerns about her son? Made her feel like she was overreacting when her son had suffered from cancer, one of the worst things a parent could face in regards to their child?

"You don't have to thank me. I'm just glad that he's healthy. That's the best result any physician can ask for," he said.

"When he was sick, I imagined him growing up. Going to college, getting married, having children of his own. I thought about him being a rebellious teenager, sneaking out of the house at night to see his girlfriend. Or boyfriend." She smiled, lost in thought. "I celebrated when he misbehaved. Weird, right? But that meant he had the energy to disobey. I prayed so many nights that I'd get the chance to see him grow up and see him do good things. And maybe a few bad, but not too many. A mother has to draw the line somewhere."

"Considering his history, when he was diagnosed, and his prognosis now, there's no reason he won't grow up to be that annoying teenager." Harrison grinned. "But maybe don't wish for a teenager who sneaks out of the house. I did that and my mom tanned my hide when I got home. One time I was grounded for an entire month."

She clucked her tongue. "Who would've thought the revered Dr. Thornton would've been such a naughty teenage boy?"

"Oh, you have no idea how naughty I can be." He couldn't stop the growl lacing those words, and when he saw her eyes widen, he felt like he could conquer the world.

She was attracted to him, that was more than apparent. If he played his cards right, they could both get some enjoyment out of this insane chemistry brimming between them.

"Harrison, how have you been?" A man shouted from across the restaurant, and Harrison watched as a very drunk Devin Yates —once a good friend, now more of a town annoyance—stumbled over to their table.

Harrison had to restrain himself from tossing Devin across the room, especially when he finally noticed Sara and exclaimed, "Sara Flannigan! Jesus Christ, seriously?" For whatever reason, he thought that was hilarious, and he started laughing so loudly that they were attracting stares.

Harrison saw Sara flush in anger. Did she even remember Devin? He vaguely remembered that they would've been in high school around the same time.

"Shit, I haven't seen you in forever," Devin continued as he stared at Sara. "How's it going? You still up to your old tricks? Man, the stories we'd hear about you! You were a legend."

Harrison stilled. "Devin, you're drunk," he said in a slow voice, venom lacing the words. "You should leave."

"Aw, come on. You knew about Sara? She was famous. Getting with the entire football team—"

She blanched.

"Leave. Leave, now, before I make you." Harrison's voice was low, threatening, as he stood up in front of Devin.

Devin blinked before he narrowed his eyes. "What the fuck, man? Don't act like you don't know. She was the town tramp—"

Devin didn't get to finish that sentence. Harrison grabbed him by the wrist and wrenched his arm behind his back. Devin swore, but Harrison just held him harder.

"I don't know what the fuck you're talking about, and I don't want to know," he hissed, anger swirling through him. "But you're going to apologize, and then you're going to leave before I leave your face permanently rearranged."

Devin struggled, but he was too drunk to put up a real fight. Finally, when he realized Harrison wasn't letting up, he said, "Fine. Sorry. You happy?"

"Look at her when you say it."

"Sorry," he sneered. "I didn't know you'd claimed the slut for yourself."

Harrison didn't think: he reacted. He hauled Devin out the door of the Fainting Goat and, slamming him against the brick wall of the restaurant, punched him in the stomach. Devin collapsed in a heap at his feet. "Go home. You're a disgrace."

Harrison turned, only to run into Trent Younger. Trent glanced over Harrison's shoulder to see Devin slumped onto the ground, moaning.

"Don't lecture me, man," Harrison replied in a tight voice.

"I wasn't going to. I was going to punch him if you weren't, but I see you did a decent job." Trent's mouth twisted. "He's a piece of shit, and has been for ages. Somebody needed to punch him."

Harrison laughed a little at that. Closing his eyes, he took a deep breath. He needed to check on Sara. Oh God, the look on her face. Anger took over once again, and it was only Trent's hand on his arm that stopped him from punching Devin a second time.

"Leave it, man. Not worth having your brother arrest you. Go take care of your date."

Entering the restaurant, Harrison didn't see Sara at their booth. Fear rushed through him until he saw that she was surrounded by some of the patrons and waitresses near the bar. Her face was stricken and pale. Rushing toward the group, he said, "Let's go."

Sara didn't argue. They walked past Devin staggering away, but Sara didn't say anything. He escorted her to his car and, after forcing aside the anger still boiling inside him, asked, "Are you okay?"

She wiped at her eyes. "Do you think I'm okay?"

He swore. Leaning over, he touched her face. "Devin's a piece of shit, and a drunk one at that. Don't let what he said get to you."

"You never knew, did you?" Her words were a whisper.

"What do you mean?"

But she was shaking her head. "I don't want to talk about it. Take me home. Please."

He wanted to comfort her, take her into his arms, but he put the car in drive and took her home instead.

At the front door of her small house, he couldn't stop from pulling her into his arms for a hug. She instantly wound her arms around him, and he reveled in her closeness. In her sweet scent, her warmth.

"What did you do to Devin?" she asked.

"I punched him."

He was expecting her to rebuke him, but she said simply, "Good."

As she gazed up at him, her eyes shining in the low light of the streetlamps, Harrison couldn't untangle his feelings. Protectiveness, anger, desire, joy, all swirled together until only one thought was coursing through his brain: *I need her.*

When he cupped her face in his hands, she didn't pull away. She tipped her head back, and that was all the permission he needed. He kissed her with an intensity he'd never felt before. She tasted like cider and mint, all sweetness and light. He brushed the remaining tears from her cheeks as the kiss only deepened. Licking inside her mouth, he poured everything he had into that one kiss.

She made a little noise in the back of her throat. God, she was gorgeous. He wanted her in every way a man could have a woman.

But then she broke the kiss. "It's getting late," she said, breathless.

He was already hard, straining, and the desire inside him was a veritable storm. He wanted to take her back to his house and ravish her until she was hoarse from screaming his name.

"Okay," he replied. He set her free. "I'll call you tomorrow."

"Okay." Then she stood on her tiptoes to kiss his cheek. "Thank you, for everything."

He murmured in reply, "You're welcome, Sara."

*a*pril showers brought May flowers, but on this late March Saturday, the Thornton family decided to take advantage of the rare sunshine and go out on the lake that made Fair Haven famous.

Normally Harrison enjoyed these outings: the sun, the lake, the boat, his family. Being the eldest of six siblings meant a raucous, energetic family life throughout his childhood and adolescence. Although half of his siblings—Mark, the third eldest, and the twins, Lizzie and Seth (fourth and fifth eldest, respectively)—were too far away to join most outings these days, Harrison still liked to have a beer with Caleb and catch up with the youngest of the family, Jubilee.

Today, though, he knew he was getting grilled. Their mom and the matriarch of the Thornton clan, Lisa Thornton, had gotten wind of Harrison dating Sara Flannigan and the resulting fight that had broken out at The Fainting Goat. To say that was she upset would be an understatement.

Harrison watched as Lisa pursed her lips in that way that signaled she was upset. Their dad, Dave, manned the boat as they made their way to the middle of the lake. Fair Haven was one of a number of towns in Washington that sat on or near one of the many lakes that created the Puget Sound. The sun shone down in spectacular fashion, the water now a glittering collection of reflective sunlight, while in the distance, you could see the snow capped mountains.

"She's pissed, you know," Caleb said. The brothers lounged on the deck, drinking beers and eating their mom's famous bean dip. "She heard about the fight from Teresa Anderson, of all people."

"Aw, fuck. That's just what I need in my life—gossiping busybodies like Teresa."

Caleb grinned. "It's your own fault. You really thought you could date one of the Flannigan girls without anyone freaking out? You've overset the world order. You've gone against convention. You'll have to fight to the death to defend your honor—"

Harrison glared at his younger brother. "Shut up, Caleb."

He refused to apologize for taking Sara out. He didn't care that her family was from "the wrong side of the tracks," like this was 1915 or something. He didn't care that her mom had been a notorious alcoholic, and he didn't care that she'd married young and had a kid. Those things just gave her character. What did he want with some young chick whose most pressing issue was that she couldn't afford the latest Louis Vuitton bag?

Lisa took that moment to place another bag of chips next to the collection she'd already started for her sons. With her white-blond hair and bright blue eyes, Lisa Thornton managed to remain stunningly beautiful into her sixties. She had an icy kind of beauty that intimidated anyone who didn't really know her, but she was extremely devoted to her husband and children. She was the proverbial Tiger Mom—even when all of her children were already adults. She'd told Harrison that the day she wasn't involved in her kids' lives was the day they put her in the ground.

"Caleb, did you put on sunscreen?" she asked with a frown. "You remember the last time you got so sunburned."

Caleb made a face. "Mom, I'm fine. It's March."

"Do you think that matters? Let me go get the bottle from your father. You're both so stubborn about this." She glanced at Harrison, and he almost squirmed underneath her disapproving gaze.

Almost. He wasn't exactly some dumb kid anymore. He held Lisa's stare; she was the first one to break it.

Caleb whistled as Lisa walked away. "You are in such trouble. She might write you out of her will."

"You're enjoying this, aren't you?"

"Are you kidding? Of course I am. The perfect, oldest Thornton son, doing something our parents don't like? I'm making a scrapbook of it."

Harrison gazed out onto the lake. He wished Sara would've come along, but he'd understood her decision to decline the invitation. Besides, she had a young son to care for.

Her absence didn't stop Harrison from going over that kiss over and over again, committing it to memory for all eternity. It had been a kiss that had kept him up at night the past week, a kiss that had touched something deep inside himself that he wasn't sure he wanted to consider.

He did, however, greatly consider getting Sara Flannigan into his bed as soon as possible.

"You're making a scrapbook? Of what?"

Jubilee, the baby of the family, bounced into the chair opposite her brothers. With her long, dark hair and light green eyes, she was already considered a beauty. At twenty-three, she'd only recently gotten her own place, although she was struggling to find employment despite her best efforts. Jubilee had been diagnosed with leukemia at the age of five, and as a result, the entire family had sheltered her. She'd suffered from various ailments, including the leukemia returning when she was thirteen. Now, though, she was healthy and thriving, albeit still sheltered.

Harrison had a difficult time imagining his baby sister as an adult. They'd had to rally around her to keep her alive for so many years that he knew it was difficult for all of them—especially his parents—to recognize that she was now a young woman.

"I'm making a scrapbook to document all of the bad things Harrison is doing to piss off our parents," Caleb responded.

Jubilee smiled. "I heard you took out Sara Flannigan. How was it? Do you like her?"

"Like I'm answering that question so you can go tell Mom," Harrison said in a wry tone.

"I would not! Now that I have my own place, Mom leaves me alone."

"She stops by every week, Jubi," Caleb said gently.

A slight flush crawled up Jubilee's cheeks. Harrison cut his brother a mean look. *Don't upset her*, he thought.

"Hey, I'm just teasing. You're doing really well. We're all happy to see you move out and get your own place. I know Mom didn't want you to." Caleb raised his beer like he was toasting her.

"You're taking care of yourself?" Harrison couldn't help but ask. Jubilee's leukemia had been the reason he'd decided to pursue medicine in the first place, and he knew all too well the statistics in regards to childhood cancers. Jubilee was healthy now, but would that last?

She rolled her eyes. "Yes, *Dad*. I'm fine. Don't hover. You're worse than Mom."

Caleb laughed while Harrison gave him the finger.

"What are you doing? Harrison, stop making such an obscene gesture. I swear, did none of you grow up? Were you raised by wolves? Here, Caleb, use this sunscreen before you're a tomato." Lisa sat down across from them, crossing her legs at the ankles. "How is it that none of you are married yet? I ask you that. I'll be dead and gone by the time you get married, and I'll never get to meet my grandchildren..."

All three Thornton kids rolled their eyes in unison. Lisa was always pestering them about marriage and grandkids—Harrison especially. At the ripe old age of thirty-four, Lisa had despaired of him ever marrying.

In a vision that stunned him, he saw Sara in a white dress, walking down the aisle. Toward him.

His heart pounded so hard that he didn't hear Lisa ask him something.

What was that about? he wondered.

"Harrison, are you listening to me?"

He turned toward Lisa to see her frowning at him. "What?"

"Really. You're the worst of all. Going on dates with women like *her* and getting into *brawls*. It's enough to make a mother lose her mind."

Jubilee patted Lisa on the knee. "Don't worry, Mom. You have five other kids to make you proud."

Caleb snorted, but it became a cough when Harrison kicked him.

"I just don't see why you would take out a woman like Sara Flannigan," Lisa complained. "She's no good for you, Harrison. Why, you got into a fight with someone on your first date! Do you think that's normal?"

Harrison gritted his teeth. "Devin Yates is an asshole and I'm glad I punched him. He deserved it, for what he called Sara."

He hadn't told his family what Devin had said, although he had a feeling that if they hadn't heard from someone else, they would eventually. That was what happened in a town of this size: no secrets were ever kept secrets for long. He didn't want to humiliate Sara further by telling other people the horrible names Devin had called her.

Lisa's eyes widened. "Language! And if this is how you behave when you're with her... I have to say, your father and I won't support you in this, Harrison."

Harrison had had enough. He said in a low voice, "I don't need your approval, Mother. I'm a grown man. Who I date is none of your concern. I would highly recommend that you keep your nose out of my business."

Lisa looked like she wanted to argue, but instead, she rose from her chair and went to find Dave. Silence reigned for a moment, and Harrison wondered if his siblings agreed with Lisa.

"Shit," Caleb finally said, whistling. "I've never seen you get this worked up over a woman."

"And I think it's great," Jubilee interrupted. "If you like her, you should date her. Don't listen to Mom. You know how she is. She's just protective."

Harrison smiled at his little sister. "You'd think she'd be more understanding."

"You'd think that." Caleb tipped back his beer. "But maybe she's just afraid of the same thing happening to you."

It made a twisted kind of sense, Harrison thought. Lisa Thornton had come from the infamous Harrison clan, and Dave Thornton had flouted convention and family approval when he'd married Lisa. Harrison's paternal grandparents had shunned them for over a decade. Lisa had faced all manner of discrimination, and more than likely, none of them had any idea the scope of how bad it had been.

Harrison's anger at his mother remained, but it lost its edge. He blew out a breath. "I should go talk to her."

"Let her calm down. Dad will pull her away from the ledge." Caleb rifled around in the nearby cooler for another beer. "You guys want anything?"

Jubilee took a beer, which raised eyebrows. She raised her chin. "I'm legal!"

"That's not the issue," Harrison said. "We just thought you hated beer."

"Well, I'm branching out. Trying new things." Opening the

beer, she slugged the drink so quickly that she ended up coughing. Harrison patted her on the back.

Jubilee eventually left to find their parents, leaving Harrison and Caleb to themselves. They sat in silence as they watched the sun move across the sky, the breeze getting colder as the day passed. Harrison almost commented that Caleb should've used that sunscreen, as his nose was already red. But maybe that was the eternal struggle of parents: they could advise and cajole and command and punish until the end of time, but they couldn't make their children into the exact image they thought was best no matter how hard they tried.

"Do you really like her?" Caleb asked. He didn't have to clarify who.

Harrison tipped his head back in the chair. "Yeah, I do."

Caleb didn't respond for a few moments. Finally: "Then you should date her. Even though I think you're insane, you know. The Flannigan girls are dangerous."

Harrison didn't correct his brother. The Flannigans *were* dangerous, but not in the way Caleb had meant.

SARA PLACED the bowl of salad on the kitchen table and began to serve James. He made a face at the mounting pile of lettuce on his plate, but he'd learned that complaining only caused him to have to eat more vegetables.

"James, eat some salad first, then lasagna. And don't make that face." Sara began to serve Ruth, but Ruth took the bowl from her to serve herself.

It had been a week since her date with Harrison Thornton. When she'd come home with red eyes and tear-streaked makeup, Ruth had demanded that she tell her what had happened.

Although Sara had assured her mother that she hadn't cried over Harrison, Ruth hadn't been particularly convinced.

It was ironic, really, that the parent that hadn't even known about Sara's ordeals in high school was suddenly trying to protect her as an adult. Sara swallowed the acidic replies that she wanted to say to her mother, replies that Megan would've thrown at Ruth without even considering the repercussions.

Sara hadn't told Megan what had happened. She didn't need her sister blowing things out of proportion. Besides, it was over, and Sara could focus on Harrison.

Harrison. They texted daily, flirty notes that sent her heart pounding. And that kiss! She'd never forget that kiss. She'd never been kissed like that—like she was the reason for a man to breathe. A kiss that had gone all the way to her toes and lodged in her very soul.

"Mom, can I have a breadstick?" James's puppy-dog eyes were so pathetic that Sara couldn't help but laugh.

"Sure—but just one to start! You'll get so full on bread you won't eat the rest of your dinner."

He ripped into a breadstick with the energy only a six-year-old boy could manage. Ruth ate her dinner in silence, except for the occasional glances she sent her daughter. Ruth thought that Sara should stop this *thing* with Harrison, because the Thorntons were "never up to anything good."

Why was everyone determined to see them parted? Sara didn't get it. It was like some bad melodrama, which only gave her more of a reason to continue dating him. Not to mention that she couldn't stop thinking about him, or dreaming about him, or—

"Are you going to see him again?" Ruth stabbed a piece of lettuce.

"Who are you going to see?" James asked.

Sara rubbed her temples. "Nobody you need to worry about,

sweetheart." Turning to Ruth, she added, "And yes, I am. We already discussed this."

Ruth harrumphed. Pouring herself a glass of water, she looked like she wanted to say something else. Sara glared at her, gesturing at James. *Don't do this in front of him*, she thought. The last thing she needed was to explain this whole thing to her son.

James finished and asked to be excused. Sara agreed, telling him that he could watch TV for an hour before bed.

Now alone with Ruth, Sara stared at her plate and couldn't find the energy to finish her food. But out of sheer stubbornness, she ate another bite of lasagna. And another. She wasn't going to avoid living her life just because other people didn't approve of everything she did.

"You really think this is going to go anywhere?" Ruth asked in a low voice. "That a Thornton is going to take one of us seriously?"

Sara clenched her jaw. "So you're saying I'm not good enough for him?"

"No, the opposite. He's not good enough for *you*. I know those Thorntons: they think they rule the town, and that everyone has to do what they say. Even if this boy of yours is a good egg, his parents sure as hell aren't. They'll make your life hell just because they can."

Sara drank the rest of her water. She was practically vibrating with anger—not only at Ruth, but at the circumstances. She did know how the Thorntons operated, and she knew that they wouldn't rally around someone like her. They'd turn up their noses, citing the past, saying that she wasn't good enough for their precious son.

"I don't care what they think," Sara finally said. At Ruth's look, she said in a firm voice, "I don't. We're adults. He doesn't care about my family"—at that, Ruth flinched—"and I don't care about his. We're only dating, anyway. We aren't secretly betrothed. Everyone needs to calm down."

"I agree, but I'm just trying to keep you safe. I don't want to see you hurt. I know what Kyle did to you—"

At that, Sara held up a hand. She did not need to talk about her failed marriage right now. "Just stop, okay? Stop trying to make up for my childhood by being overbearing now. It's not going to work."

The words fell from her lips before she could stop them, and she instantly regretted them. Ruth turned pale. Her lips thin, she stood and picked up the plates to carry to the kitchen.

Sara slumped in her chair. *Way to go, Sara.* Ruth would be pissed at her for days, even if what she'd said was the truth. She loved her mother—she did—but there was still a world of hurt they'd never worked through.

Sara considered apologizing now, but hearing Ruth bang pots and pans in the kitchen, she decided she'd wait until her mother wasn't so angry. Getting up, she carried the rest of the dirty dishes to the sink, setting them without a word for Ruth to wash. They had a deal: Sara cooked and Ruth did the dishes. This time, she didn't even look at Sara.

Fine, if she wanted to act that way, Sara would let her. She went to the living room, where James was laughing at some cartoon. Sitting on the couch, she pulled him into her arms and smelled his little boy scent: sweat and soap. She loved that scent. He snuggled into her arms, all elbows and warmth, and she said a little prayer of thanks that she got to hold him like this after everything they'd been through.

6

"*H*arrison, look alive!" Caleb tossed the basketball to his brother with an annoyed look.

Harrison caught the ball just in time. His teeth flashed in a grin, and he smiled even wider when he made a three-pointer right over Caleb's head.

"What were you saying?" Harrison asked. "Or are you all talk like you usually are?"

This afternoon, just a day after going out on the lake with the family, Caleb and Harrison had decided they needed to blow off some steam by playing ball. They'd invited Heath and their friend Jason, but the latter hadn't been able to get off work. Despite the odd number, they played a few lopsided games as the afternoon waned on.

Caleb dribbled the ball down the court. Right now, it was Harrison and Caleb versus Heath. Heath blocked Caleb as he tried to throw the ball to Harrison again, and when Caleb threw and Heath hit the ball down, Heath let out a shout of triumph as he took the ball back down the opposite side of the court.

"Like I said—what were you saying?" Harrison teased.

Caleb just flipped him off.

By three o'clock, they were sweaty and taking a quick water break, discussing whether or not they wanted another game or wanted to go to the bar early. As the weather was decent once again, they all decided to play one more game. This time, Harrison would be on his own.

He tried not to think about Sara as he played, but it was inevitable. She was always in his thoughts. This morning, when he'd texted and asked her about another date, she'd texted the worst response possible: *Maybe. I'll let you know.*

What the hell did that mean? Harrison clenched his jaw as he stole the ball from Heath and ran down to the basket. But just as he was about to shoot, Caleb jumped and caught the ball from him with a triumphant laugh.

Heath and Caleb scored once again, and it was currently eight to five, with the duo in the lead.

"You lagging, old man?" Caleb tailed Harrison as he dribbled. "You need a break?"

Harrison just turned in a quick move before shooting from the key. The ball went straight through the hoop with a swish. Cocking an eyebrow at his brother, Harrison didn't have to say anything.

When Heath dribbled the ball down the court and attempted to shoot, Harrison blocking it, Caleb said suddenly, "What the hell are they doing here?"

Harrison turned, and then promptly wondered if he were hallucinating. But given the look in Sara Flannigan's eyes as she gazed at them, he knew it wasn't any dream.

She was with her sister and James. James had his fingers in the holes of the chain link fence surrounding the outdoor basketball court, his eyes wide. He bounced on the balls of his feet.

"Break?" Harrison didn't even wait for a response as he jogged over to the Flannigans, stepping out onto the sidewalk. Megan made a face, but she stepped off to the side with her arms crossed without saying anything.

"Hey," he said, suddenly aware of how sweaty—and probably smelly—he was. He wiped his face with his shirt, but that was sweaty, as well. Sara seemed to stifle a smile at the gesture.

"Hey, James, how are you?" Harrison leaned down so he was eye level with him. "Do anything fun lately?"

James shrugged. "Just school. Sometimes I play outside with my friend Travis. Do you know Travis?"

Harrison shook his head. "But maybe I can meet him someday."

"You should. He's really good at finding grasshoppers."

Sara's stifled smile finally broke through, and Harrison felt like his entire world shifted on its axis. How could one woman manage to overset him like this? And just from a smile?

"We were taking a walk," she said, as if he had suspected they were spying on them. "But don't stop playing on our account."

He heard a snort from Megan, but he ignored it. "We were about to break anyway."

"And Harrison was losing, by the way," Caleb said as he approached, Heath behind them. "So that's probably why he wanted to go home."

"My charming brother is trying to say that he's happy to see you all, and that he would also like to introduce Heath to you if you haven't met him already." Harrison gave Caleb a look.

Heath, behind Caleb, grinned. "No need. Sara and I both know each other from school."

Of course they did—how could Harrison have forgotten that? And then the next thought: did Heath have his eye on Sara? Why wouldn't he? Any heterosexual man in the general vicinity would be blind not to want her. It was stupid for him to worry about Heath's interest considering the kiss they'd recently shared. But jealousy wasn't known for its adherence to logic.

"How are you, Sara? James? You ready for school tomorrow?" Heath asked.

"No, but I will be. I'm ready for all of this standardized testing to be done, though. My kids looked like they were going to start crying on Friday when I said we weren't done yet."

Heath laughed, which just made Harrison grit his teeth.

"My kids reacted the same way," Heath said. But then he seemed to notice Harrison's expression, and he cleared his throat. "Hey, Caleb, let's go get a drink."

Harrison turned slightly to see Caleb glaring at Megan Flannigan. But not just glaring—if Harrison didn't know better, he'd say his brother were looking at Megan with lust. Pure, unadulterated, I-need-you-right-now kind of desire.

The kind of desire he felt for Sara right this second.

Caleb shook himself; Megan blushed and looked away.

"Yeah, a drink. We'll see you later, Harrison."

As the men walked to their cars, Megan said, "James, let's go to the park and play. Your mom will join us in a bit." She raised an eyebrow at Sara in question. "Right?"

Sara nodded. She and Harrison watched those two leave—and Harrison noticed that Megan walked in the same direction as Caleb and Heath—and then it was just them. Alone. Standing together.

He wanted to ask her why she replied the way she had to his text, but mostly he wanted to curl a finger around a strand of her hair. He wanted to taste her again. God, he just *wanted* her. Maybe she thought they shouldn't date, though, considering what had happened last time. The memory of Devin Yates sparked anger in his gut. If he saw that asshole again, he'd punch him again. In multiple places.

He needed to convince Sara not to throw away what they had. Whatever it was. Even if it was just a fling. Although at the idea that this would end, Harrison felt his heart constrict. *Why do I care so much already?*

SARA COULD BARELY LOOK at Harrison. Not because she didn't want to—she wanted to. She had watched how he'd played ball with his brother and friend, his sweaty shirt sticking to his abdomen and delineating his muscles. Standing in front of her, he smelled like raw masculinity, and she had to restrain herself from burying her nose against him. He looked so *potent*, so capable. If she weren't careful, she'd do something very stupid right this moment.

"Go out with me tonight," Harrison said in a low voice. His green eyes were dark, and she became lost in them. "Let me go home and I'll pick you up later."

She hesitated. Oh, she wanted to. She wanted to so badly that she felt it in her bones. But after Megan had found out about what had happened on their first date, Sara had wondered if she were in over her head. Did she want to fight against everyone in this town to be with Harrison Thornton? Did she want to experience the inevitable sneers and comments from not only his family, but from other people?

A huge part of her wanted to say yes. She wanted not to care. She wanted to fall into whatever this was and never look back. But she had James to think of. What if her actions with Harrison made James's life harder? What if he were teased at school? Or worse?

She swallowed. She watched as a bead of sweat trailed down Harrison's tanned throat, and she wanted to lick it. She wanted to taste the salt of his skin, and feel his hands all over her body.

"I'm not sure that's a good idea," she hedged.

"Why not?"

She almost laughed at his frankness, but he wasn't laughing. "Because of what happened last time." When Harrison just looked at her, she added, "You know what I mean. You know who I am, and who you are. We can't change that. What if we're just making drama for no reason?"

A flash of anger crossed his face, and she could see how quick his temper could be once again. The same temper that had defended her against Devin Yates. She shivered, although not from fear. From want.

"I don't care what your last name is, and I don't care what mine is, either," he said in a low voice. He stepped closer to her. "And I have a feeling you don't care. Not really. Do you really want pieces of shit like Devin to dictate how we live?"

She had to tilt her head back to look at him. Steeling herself, she explained, "This isn't about having anyone dictate to us, but recognizing when we can't change the facts. That's all that I'm saying."

She didn't know why she was saying these things. Did she want to end things, now? Her heart splintered at the thought. *Tell me I'm wrong*, she pleaded. *Tell me I'm worth the fight.*

Harrison touched her cheek. "I think you're afraid. I don't say that as an insult, though. If I'm being honest, I am, too. But we can't let fear control us." Brushing a strand of hair from her face, he said, "Go out with me, Sara. Just one more date. That's it."

She swallowed. His fingers were like brands against her cheek. She wanted to close her eyes, lean into that touch.

She wrestled with what she wanted to do, and what she should do. When she'd been younger, she'd always done what she needed to do. Care for Megan, do well in school. It was only when she'd met Kyle that she'd experienced what doing what you wanted could be like. That had ended disastrously. So should she give in, once more, to what she wanted? Even though the logical part of her mind had a feeling it couldn't end well, no matter how much she wanted it to?

Harrison brushed this thumb over her bottom lip. That simple touch sparked through her entire body. But he didn't stop: he traced down her throat, circling in the dip of her collarbone. He leaned toward her. To her dismay, he didn't kiss her—at least not on the lips. He brushed a kiss to her shoulder, so warm and gentle that tears almost sprang to her eyes.

"Go out with me," he said a third time.

She swallowed. His kiss burned on her shoulder.

"Okay," she said. "I'll go out with you again."

"Mom, look!"

Sara ignored Megan's glare as she watched her son. He climbed on the monkey bars, hanging one-handed before jumping to the ground below. In a quick move, he clambered on top of the bars, almost falling in the process.

"Please don't break anything!" she called. She really didn't need to take James to the ER because of a broken arm.

"So, what happened?" Megan sidled up to Sara and poked her in her side. "By the look on your face, it was something good."

Sara refused to blush. "We're going out again. Tonight."

"Huh. Well, I hope it goes better this time than the last."

James decided that the monkey bars were no longer interesting and decided to move to the swings. To Sara's amusement, he tried to put together two swings so he could lie down on them, but when he had no one to push him, he yelled, "Come help me!"

"James, swing normally. Don't give me that look. Otherwise we're going home."

He huffed but did as Sara told him, sitting on his bum in the swing and pumping his legs, his expression one of resignation that his mother was so very boring.

"I've decided I'm going to enjoy myself and not care what other people think," Sara replied. "And that includes you, dear sister."

Megan held up her hands. "Hey, I've been totally nice. Okay, slightly nice. But you know how I feel about that family. They're trouble."

"No, you're trouble. You were the one who got arrested, remember?"

Megan scowled, a blush tingeing her cheeks. Sara never mentioned The Incident, but today, she'd lost patience with her sister. Her dislike of the Thorntons—namely, Caleb Thornton—wasn't going to influence Sara's decision to date the eldest Thornton.

"And Caleb Thornton hasn't let me forget what happened," Megan snapped. "He constantly rubs it in my face. He acts like I murdered his grandmother, the way he looks at me."

"Oh Megan. I know you can be hardheaded, but have you ever thought that maybe he's *interested* in you but just doesn't know how to show it?"

"What, because he's in kindergarten and can only pull my hair? If he is interested—which he is *not*, by the way—then he should put on his big boy pants and do something about it."

"Considering you'd rip his arm off if he tried, I doubt he'll do anything about it."

Megan glared at Sara, but the glare soon turned into a wry laugh. Megan pulled on her sister's hair, which just made Sara pull on one of Megan's braids.

"Don't change the subject," Megan accused, "we're talking about you, not me. Are you sure you know what you're doing?"

"That I'm sure I'm going on a date with a handsome man who has a job? Wow, what is wrong with me?"

Megan just tugged Sara's hair again. "Don't deflect."

Sara watched as James swung higher and higher, and he waved at her. She waved back. Did she know what she was doing? No, not really. She knew she wanted Harrison Thornton more than she'd wanted anyone in her entire life. She'd never wanted Kyle like she wanted Harrison. Kyle had been a teenage infatuation that had tried to be something more despite all of the warning signs.

"I don't know," Sara admitted. "I don't know what'll happen. But if I sit at home, twiddling my thumbs, I'll regret not trying."

Megan rubbed her arms. "You're right, even if it irritates me."

"What did I do now?"

Megan wouldn't look at her now. "You're always so brave, you know? You don't let bullshit keep you from living. Whereas sometimes I think I won't be able to get out of bed, I'm so scared." The last words were said in a whisper, and they broke Sara's heart.

She pulled her sister into a hug. "You don't have to be scared anymore. You have a great life, and a great business, and I know you'll meet a great guy. He might even be someone you'd least expect."

Megan just laughed and went to push James on the swing. Sara knew her sister wasn't much for talking about feelings or fears, so this particular admission by her was an anomaly—one that proved to Sara that Megan still needed to work through her feelings with Ruth, their childhood, her arrest at seventeen, and even her feelings toward Caleb Thornton. Sara knew that Megan blamed Caleb for more things than were actually his fault, probably because he was an easy target.

Sara sighed.

But she wasn't going to let her sister, or Harrison's siblings, or Devon Yates, or anyone else, keep her from seeing Harrison tonight. Her heart lifted, remembering the look in his eyes as he'd gazed down at her. How he'd touched her cheek, kissed her shoulder. *I'm going to sleep with him, aren't I?* she thought, rather wildly.

She laughed out loud, but covered her mouth so Megan wouldn't hear her. The only man she'd ever slept with was Kyle, and she'd gotten pregnant with James after only two months together. Sex had always been something she'd had to do to keep Kyle interested. Beyond that, she'd found it uneventful, if not downright unlikeable. She'd always blamed herself for that, but with her desire for Harrison coursing through her veins, she wondered for the first time if it hadn't been her fault at all.

Her thoughts about Harrison scattered when James jumped from the swing while up in the air. Her heart caught in her throat, seeing him fall that far, and she expected the worst when she ran up to him. Megan was already there, checking him, but he just lay on his back and laughed.

"Did you see that? I was so high!" He laughed at his mom and aunt's expressions.

"James Arthur Flannigan, you almost gave me a heart attack!" Sara pulled him into a hug, which he allowed for about one and a half seconds before wiggling free.

"I'm fine! Let's go on the slide!"

But Sara caught him by the hand and said, "No way, mister. After that stunt, we're going home." James started to whine, but she leaned down to speak to him at eye level. "No whining. I have somewhere to go tonight. I bet your aunt Megan will have dinner with you and Grandma, though. Won't you, Megan?"

Megan had had no intention of hanging with their mother, but she shrugged. "Sure, why not? What else do I have to do?" She grabbed James's hand and they marched down the street, Sara shaking her head and smiling at the pair as they returned home.

a s Sara was debating whether to wear a nude shade of lipstick or the brighter red, she heard her phone ring. She didn't recognize the number, so she let it go to voicemail, assuming it was more than likely a spam call. But when her phone alerted her that the caller had left a voicemail, she gave into curiosity and listened to the message.

"Ms. Daniels, this is Vincent Elan with Elan, Farraday and Rothschild. I'm calling on behalf of my client Mr. Kyle Daniels. He is concerned about your potentially violating your custody agreement in regards to your son, James Daniels, and will be pursuing legal action if necessary. Please have your lawyer contact me as soon as possible."

Sara placed her phone back on her vanity slowly, her heart pounding so hard she felt dizzy. The array of emotions attempting to flood through her—fear, anger, shock—made her unable to process what she'd just heard. Then the single, terrifying thought: *Kyle's going to take James from me.*

She covered her mouth to stifle the noise that almost burst forth. Anxiety engulfed her. Putting her head between her knees, she told herself to keep calm. This was all posturing, nothing more. Kyle wanted to punish her for leaving Seattle and taking James with her. He had no interest in becoming a full-time father. She knew that, logically, but her emotions swirled until she wasn't sure if she was going to cry or vomit. Maybe both. Forcing herself to take deep breaths, she finally got herself calm enough to think clearly.

She needed to contact her lawyer. She didn't have the money to afford him a second time, not after the divorce, but what could she do? She couldn't let Kyle take James. He didn't care about his own son, at least not beyond using him to punish Sara for daring to leave Kyle in the first place. *And of course he makes sure I'm called Sara Daniels*, she thought bitterly. *I'll be eighty-five and Kyle will still make sure to call me by his last name.*

"Sara, are you ready? Harrison just drove up," Ruth called from the living room.

Harrison! She'd forgotten about their date in her distress over the phone call from Kyle's lawyer. Oh God, how could she go on a date with him when the thought of leaving James behind sent her into absolute terror? What if Kyle showed up and took him?

She rubbed her temples. She couldn't get hysterical. Kyle wasn't going to kidnap James, because that would take effort. Kyle had never been interested in putting in effort. James would be perfectly safe here with Ruth and Megan. Besides, Megan would punch Kyle if he got near James.

That image put a small smile on her face. Looking in the mirror, she decided to go with the red lipstick, because she needed to put on a brave face. Maybe the lipstick would be like a mask, keeping her emotions from spilling over during dinner. Because for whatever reason, she didn't want to tell Harrison her ex-husband was harassing her. How humiliating! Not only was she the victim of Devin Yates's harassment, but her own ex-husband wouldn't leave her alone, either. The thought of Harrison pitying her was almost too much to bear.

She grabbed her purse and came into the living room just as she heard a knock on the door. James jumped up to grab the door before she could say anything.

"Oh! It's you. Why are you here?" James made a face.

Harrison, looking dashing in a dark green button-up and dark slacks, laughed. "Hey, buddy. I'm here for your mom." His gaze shifted to Sara, and it instantly heated.

"Where are you guys going?" James asked, his eyebrows furrowed.

Sara leaned down to kiss him on the cheek, which promptly left a red lipstick print. "Be good for your grandma and aunt. I'll be back after you go to sleep."

He nodded, but not before he looked at Harrison suspiciously. Sara had to bite back a laugh; it didn't help that James still had the bright red lipstick print on his cheek.

"Have a good time," Megan called. Megan had decided to stay the evening, although she and Ruth hadn't spoken much. Ruth felt awkward around her youngest daughter, while Megan had told Sara that she had a difficult time saying anything nice to their mother.

Before Harrison opened the passenger door for her, he drank her in with his eyes—from her dark pink wrap dress to her heels to her racy display of cleavage. "You look beautiful. If your son weren't looking out the window right now, I'd kiss you."

She smiled, blushing a little. When she saw James peering at them through the curtains, she laughed. "He's a bit of a peeping tom. Unless you want him to show you his roly-poly collection, we'd better head off."

"I'm tempted, but I'll have to decline the bug showing for tonight."

"Too bad. It's a pretty epic collection."

Harrison drove them to Fair Haven's downtown, parking a block away from the Italian restaurant Angelo's that had recently opened. The sun had already set, although it was just warm enough not to need a sweater. She had a feeling Harrison would keep her warm no matter the season, though.

They sat at a candlelit table, ordering a bottle of the best red wine. Harrison gazed at her across from the table, and Sara had to stop herself from blushing like a teenager. He managed to give her his whole attention, something she'd never experienced with any other man. Usually they got distracted with their phones, or they got bored talking about whatever it was Sara wanted to talk about. The few dates she'd gone on since her divorce had made her realize that few men wanted to listen to a woman talk about her young son the entire time they were out. But James was her entire world. If these men didn't understand that from the beginning, then they weren't worth her time.

"How have you been?" Harrison asked.

She smiled. "Since I saw you four hours ago? Just fine."

"Only fine? That's a shame. I went home and thought about you the entire time."

"Such a flirt. Would it hurt your feelings if I said I thought about laundry, dinner, and James, in that order?"

He snorted. "You do know how to burst a man's ego. That's all right, though. I like a challenge."

She sipped her wine as she looked at him over the rim. The candlelight gave his chiseled face additional edges while somehow softening them as well. He looked entirely too kissable in this environment. When she felt his foot touching her calf, she had to bite back a laugh.

"Sir, is that your foot? Keep your feet to yourself, like I tell my son all the time."

He just rubbed her calf with his foot, which made her body heat. "Good thing I'm not a six-year-old boy."

"Yes," she admitted in a whisper.

Their appetizers arrived, and Sara found herself famished.

She'd been too busy today to eat more than some yogurt. As she munched on bruschetta, though, she wondered if she had mints in her bag. *Yes, and gum.* Good, because this bruschetta had enough garlic to smell from a mile away.

"Tell me what else you did today." Harrison gave her the last bruschetta. "What does Sara Flannigan do for fun?"

"For fun? I don't have much time for fun. I work, I take care of my kid, and I sleep. Sometimes I go to the grocery store." She shrugged. "I'm boring."

"I doubt that."

"What about you? What does a famous, talented doctor do when he's not saving lives?"

"Would it surprise you that I also do laundry and go to the grocery store?"

She gasped. "You don't have servants for that?"

"No, because I'm not Prince William. I even did my own laundry as a kid."

Her eyebrows lifted. "Now, that does surprise me."

"My mom had too many kids to do everything herself, and then when Jubilee got sick..." He trailed off, clearly lost in memories.

Sara had forgotten that one of his siblings had been sick. Had it also been cancer, like James?

"She had leukemia," Harrison explained, based on her questioning glance. "Around the same age as James. The cancer returned when she was thirteen, though. She's healthy now, but it was a struggle for the whole family, to see our baby sister so sick."

Her heart clenched at his words. "But she's okay now?"

"Very. She just got her own place and she's as annoying as she's ever been." He smiled. "She was the reason I wanted to be a doctor in the first place, and an oncologist specifically."

"I'm glad she's healthy now. I hate that we're both a part of the same club, but it's nice to know someone else on the inside."

He lifted his wine glass. "A toast: to our family members who kicked cancer's ass."

She raised her glass in return. "I can always toast to that."

They clinked glasses, and Sara couldn't help the laugh that burst forth. Harrison gave her a look full of fiery promise, but when their waiter filled their water glasses, the look turned to a heated simmer.

"Jubilee is looking for a job. You know of any place that's hiring, let me know," he said as their waiter walked away.

Sara considered, and then a light bulb went off in her head. "You should send her to my sister's bakery. Megan's employee Daria is going to be taking off for maternity leave soon, and although it would be a temporary position, I know Megan mentioned that Daria is on the fence whether or not she'll stay home for good with the baby or not."

"That would be perfect. I'll let Jubi know. I can't say that she knows much about cash registers or making cinnamon rolls, but she's a quick learner."

"Considering Megan didn't know anything about running a business until a year ago...I'd say your sister will be fine."

He laughed. "Sounds perfect then. Although I'll tell Caleb to leave Megan alone so she doesn't poison him."

"That's probably a good idea. Those two are always at each other's throats."

They chatted and laughed as the evening passed, and Sara couldn't help but practically inhale the delicious food set in front of her. By the time dessert arrived, she had protested that she couldn't eat another bite, but the chocolate torte was too tempting. She dug in and couldn't stop herself from moaning at the burst of chocolate on her tongue.

"You keep making that noise, and I'm going to haul you out of here and into my backseat," Harrison said in a low voice.

She couldn't help but make him suffer a little: she ate the torte slowly, making sure to lick her lips and make noises in her throat. She offered him a bite, which he took, his eyes dark with desire.

By the time she'd licked the fork clean, Harrison had called for the check. He paid and pulled Sara up from her chair.

"Let's go."

By the time they arrived at his car, he'd pressed her against it. His mouth descended onto hers before she could draw a breath. He tasted like chocolate and desire, and she clutched at his shoulders. His hips pressed against her, and feeling his hardness against her belly, desire pooled low in her stomach.

"Come back to my place," he said. "I need you, Sara."

She wanted to say yes. His tongue delved inside her mouth, and she felt like she was being consumed. Her entire body was made of fire, burning for this man who kissed like a devil sent to tempt her.

She was about to say yes when her phone rang. Harrison broke the kiss, but he didn't move away from her.

"Do you need to get that?"

She shook her head, pulling him down for another kiss. But her phone rang again, and then a third time. Groaning in frustration, she reached into her bag to see who had decided to ruin this night for her.

When she saw that Kyle was the one calling her, she cursed him to a fiery death. How dare he hound her when he had already had his lawyer threaten her hours earlier?

"What is it? You're as pale as a ghost." Harrison touched her arm.

Sara shook herself. The magic of the moment dispelled, and she wanted to stomp her feet in frustration. "No, James is fine. It's my ex. He's..." She grimaced. "Never mind. You don't want to hear about my ex-husband. Talk about a mood killer."

"Considering you looked as pale as death seeing his name on

your phone, I want to hear about him so I can get his address and pummel him."

She laughed. "Is this becoming a theme for our dates? We go to dinner, you punch a man, we kiss?"

His answering grin warmed her. "Hey, I never said things would be boring. But seriously, do you want to talk about it?"

Part of her wanted to talk about it. Part of her wanted a shoulder to cry on, a person to lean on. She'd been on her own for so long that the idea that she could rely on someone else was heady. But did she want to burden Harrison with her ex-husband's drama?

Suddenly, exhaustion swamped her, and she wanted to cry. It was stupid, but she felt like this entire thing with Harrison was hopeless. She had her ex-husband wanting custody of their son. How could she think about dating during a time like this?

She turned away. "I think I should go home."

"Why?"

"Because this isn't going to work. It just won't." She bit her lip. "I'm sorry. My life is a mess right now. You don't need to be dragged into it."

She waited to hear recriminations or accusations of leading him on. That would be how Kyle would've responded. *I've taken you out twice, shouldn't I get something, too?* But she should've known Harrison Thornton wouldn't be like that.

"Sara, come here." He enveloped her in his arms, and she couldn't stop herself from nestling against him. "You don't have to talk if you don't want to, but I'm not going to let you go home and be sad. That asshole doesn't deserve the satisfaction."

She inhaled his scent—sandalwood and cedar. He was so warm and solid that she wanted to believe he could protect her from everything life would throw at her. What would it be like to have a partner in life who supported you as much as you supported him? She'd never had that. Kyle had expected her to take care of him, but not vice versa.

"Do you want to talk about it?" Harrison asked again.

She considered. She brushed her cheek against the soft cotton of his shirt, and she couldn't stop herself from tilting her head back to look into his eyes. He had lovely eyes: bright green, like jade. Stubble dotted his cheeks and jaw, and he had a slight dimple in his chin.

He was beautiful.

"No, I don't want to talk." Before her nerve failed her, she added, "I want you to kiss me and make me forget."

Those green eyes gleamed. "Are you sure?"

She nodded. He didn't need to be asked twice.

He kissed her, his mouth gentle. He sipped from her lips, like he couldn't get enough of her. Her heart almost burst from her chest, and she moaned his name. Her emotions were careening wildly, from sheer desire to unmitigated joy. Her heart beat in her ears, her wrists, her core. If he touched her where she wanted him the most, she'd detonate with a single stroke.

"I need you, baby." He unlocked the car, opening the backseat. Before she realized it, she was underneath him on the black leather seat.

At her look, he smiled. "Don't worry. Tinted windows."

"Do you do this often?" she teased, running her fingers through his dark hair.

"If I said no, would you believe me?"

"Maybe. How about you kiss me again to convince me?"

His mouth captured hers, and their hands were just as busy. Sara caressed his muscled chest while he pushed her dress up her thighs. She was stupidly glad that it was warm enough not to wear tights, as that left her legs bare and allowed him easy access.

His fingers were like brands on her skin. She shifted beneath him, wanting him to touch her like she'd never wanted anything else. Kissing her still, he caressed her thigh, the inside of her thigh, just barely skimming where her hip met her leg.

"You're so soft," he said before kissing her throat. He licked the skin there. "I've wanted to do this since the first time I saw you."

She released a breathy moan, especially when his fingers danced closer to her sex. She knew she was wet and needy for him. As he kissed her shoulder, her collarbone, his fingers delved beneath the elastic of her panties.

"So wet already? Fuck, baby. You want me that badly?"

She nodded eagerly, pushing against his fingers. He played with her damp curls before he parted her. When he touched her sex, they both groaned. She was already trembling, and she had to grip his shoulders to keep from dissolving into a puddle of goo.

"Harrison, please," she begged as he petted her.

"Where do you want me to touch you? Tell me. I want to hear you say it."

She stilled. Their gazes locked, and swallowing, she murmured, "Touch me. Please."

"Here?" His thumb grazed her swollen clit.

She arched upward. "More, more."

He played and stroked, his thumb just barely touching her clit. Her entire body was like a live wire, building with electricity. She wondered if she were going to burst into flames. She was so close, but she couldn't get there quite yet. She moaned in frustration.

"I can feel you getting wetter. You're so hot, so beautiful." He leaned up and kissed her. "Tell me what you want, Sara."

She blushed furiously, but she was too desperate, too crazed for release. Panting, she said, "Touch my clit." He did, and she moaned. "Harder. Yes, God, like that."

He groaned too, grinding against her. When he pushed a finger inside of her, her sheath clenched around the digit just as his thumb pushed harder on her clit. The combination of his rubbing thumb and thrusting finger sent her into a hurricane of desire. She arched her hips, and he kissed her, with lips and teeth and tongue.

She felt her orgasm hit a second before she let out a shriek that he caught with his kiss. She came and came, her body shaking like a leaf in the wind. Harrison kept kissing her and murmuring things she couldn't hear. It was like she'd gone deaf and mute for a moment from the sheer pleasure he'd given her.

It took her a minute to come back to herself. The first thing she noticed was the look on Harrison's face: satisfaction. The second thing she noticed? The windows were all foggy now.

She laughed, which made him arch an eyebrow. She pointed. "How very *Titanic* of us."

He glanced at the fogged-up window. "Hopefully with fewer icebergs," he said before kissing her. Helping her sit up, he assisted her with setting her clothes to rights, although that didn't stop him from kissing her and touching her.

She never wanted to leave. If she could, she'd live in this very backseat with Harrison Thornton and never look back. It was such a silly idea that she almost laughed again.

But inevitably, reality reared its head again. She needed to go home—it was late, it was a school night. She had James. She had to figure out what she was going to do with Kyle. Sighing, she rested her head against Harrison's shoulder.

"I should get home," she murmured into the quiet.

"You sure?"

She nodded. "But thank you for tonight. And nobody got punched."

"Well, the night is young," he said with a smile. "Never say never."

8

*W*hen Sara opened the door to her classroom after dropping James off at first grade, she gasped. Sitting on her desk was a huge bouquet of roses in every color imaginable. She had no idea how the flowers had gotten here before she'd unlocked her classroom—had a janitor let in the delivery person?—but she was too preoccupied with smelling the blossoms.

She didn't need to read the card to know it was from Harrison. Opening the small note tucked underneath the ribbon surrounding the vase, she read: *I can't stop thinking about you. Let me take you out again. –HT.*

Simple, short, and to the point. She smiled even wider. Touching the silky petals, she couldn't help but remember their encounter in the backseat of his car last night. She was twenty-eight years old and she'd never done anything like that in her life. With Harrison, though, she had a feeling she was going to experience a whole bevy of things for the first time.

"Secret admirer?" Heath DiMarco stopped by her door with a raised eyebrow. A fifth grade teacher, Heath had been one of the first people she'd befriended when she'd gotten this job. Handsome, good-natured, and kind, Sara had wondered how he'd managed to stay single. If she weren't falling for Harrison Thornton, she'd sign up on what she imagined was a long waiting list of women trying to catch Heath's interest.

"Not so secret," she responded, still smiling.

"Ah, I thought it would be from him."

"How do you—? Never mind. I don't want to know. You guys are as bad about gossiping as women." She shook her finger at him, although she wasn't really annoyed.

Heath laughed. "I swear Harrison hasn't said anything. But when he basically dropped everything to talk to you during our game..." He shrugged. "You'd be an idiot not to notice."

She wanted him to tell her everything he knew, but she didn't want to seem desperate. Blushing faintly, she moved the roses underneath her desk. At Heath's look, she explained, "Third graders tend to ask a lot of questions about anything new."

"True. My fifth graders are the same, especially if I were getting flowers from somebody."

She laughed. "They'd probably be confused and never stop pestering you about it."

"I'd just tell them they're from my grandmother."

They chatted for a bit longer until Heath had to go to his own room to get ready for the day. Before he left, though, he said, "I just wanted to tell you that if you're serious about all of this"—he motioned at what Sara assumed were the flowers underneath her desk—"that I support you. I know this town can be...judgmental."

At the reminder, her happiness bubble deflated somewhat. She smiled anyway, thanking him before he left. If she didn't know better, she'd think Heath were interested in her, but he acted the same around her as he did any of the other single, female teachers here at the school. From the little bit of gossip she'd heard, Heath had moved to Fair Haven five years ago, but no one really knew about his past or his family. He was the town enigma. She wondered if Harrison knew about him. She did love a bit of mystery.

Her students arrived en masse, telling her all about their weekends. The day passed quickly, although Sara struggled not to daydream about Harrison during quieter moments. During silent reading, she'd found herself so lost in her thoughts that she didn't hear her student Xavier asking her if he could go to the bathroom the first time around. She apologized, fumbling for the bathroom pass.

During the afternoon, she got a text from Megan, asking her to meet for drinks after work. The bakery closed around the same time as school ended, which was convenient when Sara needed a babysitter and Ruth was unavailable. Telling her sister she'd meet her after she'd taken James home, she made herself focus on teaching and not on Harrison Thornton or the roses that were sitting underneath her desk all day long.

~

"DR. THORNTON, your mom called and left you a message," Jackie, one of Harrison's nurses, said as he finished a patient's chart.

He sighed. "What did she want?"

"She said that she and your dad want to go out to dinner with you tonight. She said that unless you call and tell her you're unavailable, she'll see you at the Fainting Goat at six."

Jackie recited the message in a bland tone, but Harrison knew she was restraining herself from saying something sarcastic. A hard-working but blunt-speaking woman, Jackie was Harrison's best and most capable nurse, and also a loyal friend. Ten years older than him, she was married with two teenage sons, and she always had some crazy story about one or both of her kids doing something ridiculous and, as she always termed it, something "only boys as dumb as mine would do."

"Thanks, Jackie. Since I don't have plans, I guess I'm getting dinner with my parents if I like it or not."

She scrunched her nose, which he knew meant she had something else to say. He raised an eyebrow. "Do I want to know?"

"Well, I heard through the grapevine that you're dating Sara Flannigan," she said, like she were announcing that they were out of printer toner, "and I just wanted to say that she's a good egg and anyone in this town who thinks otherwise can choke."

He stifled a laugh, although it was difficult. In a serious voice, he replied, "Thank you. I appreciate that."

"I know it's none of my business, but I hate to see anyone around here judge her for her mom. And Ruth Flannigan has worked hard to get sober and has stayed sober as far as I know. People should be celebrating that, not judging her for what happened years ago."

He didn't know where this speech was coming from, but sometimes Jackie just needed to let off steam and then she'd get back to work. Luckily, she didn't have much else to say, simply telling him that his next appointment had arrived.

It had been a crazy day, with patient after patient and barely any break in between. But working with kids and getting them better never failed to be rewarding, and thus, he couldn't truly complain. He also had it easier than a lot of other physicians, as he wasn't always on-call, unless there was some major emergency. He knew ER physicians who never seemed to get a day off, even during scheduled vacations.

By the time Harrison left work, went home and changed, and headed to the Fainting Goat, he'd resigned himself to hearing his parents lecture him about his life. Well, Lisa would lecture him. Dave would keep quiet, only occasionally interjecting or tell his wife that he'd take care of something for her. Harrison loved his parents and was grateful to them for a happy childhood and adolescence, but he was also thirty-four years old. He didn't need their input, and he certainly didn't need their approval for who he was going to date.

He arrived at the Fainting Goat a few minutes after six o'clock. The restaurant was bustling, as happy hour lasted until six-thirty during the week. Looking for his parents, he frowned when he didn't see them. His parents were never late. Dave considered lack of punctuality a sin as much as stealing and probably even murder.

"Harrison? Your table is right over here," one of the waitresses told him.

He followed, still confused, when he was sat at a table with a lone woman.

"Harrison?" the woman asked as the waitress left. "I'm Kayla Long. It's nice to meet you finally."

He shook her hand. Probably only a few years younger than him, Kayla had short dark hair in a bob haircut, her lips a bright red, and when she smiled, her teeth flashed white in the light of the restaurant. Based on her interested look and how low-cut her blouse was, he wondered if she were waiting for a boyfriend to arrive.

It took him a second, but then the pieces finally clicked.

I've been set up. By my own mother.

"Yes, I'm Harrison Thornton. Nice to meet you." He was close to telling her he hadn't agreed to any kind of date, but then he felt guilty. If he left now, everyone in the restaurant would assume that Kayla had done something rude to make him run off before the date had even started. He sat down across from her.

"Look, Kayla," he began. "I have to be honest with you—"

"That you had no idea this date was going to happen?" she interrupted. At his expression, she smiled. "I could tell based on how confused you were. I did wonder how I managed to snag a date with *the* Harrison Thornton. Now I know that it was too good to be true." Her words weren't bitter, but simply practical.

He grimaced. "God, I'm sorry. My mother set this up. Which makes me sound like some guy who lives in his mom's basement, doesn't it? I swear all of my previous relationships did not involve my mother."

She laughed. "I believe you. You don't seem the type to need any help with getting a lady." She gave him a heated once-over, then smiled again. "Let me buy you a drink."

Harrison shook his head, telling her he'd buy *her* a drink for the confusion. He didn't particularly want to have a drink with this random woman, but at least no one would gossip that something terrible had gone wrong during the date. Maybe he could foist her onto another single male friend who he knew. Heath? Caleb? Kayla was certainly beautiful enough that she could manage to find a date without difficulty.

They chatted, discussing nothing more involved than their jobs, their hobbies, and how they liked Fair Haven. Harrison discovered that Kayla had moved to Fair Haven only two months ago for her job with a newly developed tech company, and that she had a dog named Gatsby that she liked to take everywhere she could. She explained that a friend of Lisa's had given her Kayla's name, and that Kayla had been told that both parties knew of the date's existence. She apologized again for the mix-up.

After their drinks, Kayla told him that she needed to get home to walk Gatsby. Harrison appreciated that she knew when to end things, and as they were about to leave, she made a joke about setting up her own dates from now on. Harrison laughed.

And then he saw Sara staring at them both from across the restaurant, her eyes wide with shock.

Alarm bells rang in his head. Before he could react, Sara had turned around and left, her sister Megan following her.

"Shit. Shit, shit, shit," he muttered. At Kayla's look, he said, "Not you. Sorry. Something came up."

"Don't apologize to me. Go after her."

Racing outside, he caught up to Sara and Megan right as they were about to get into Sara's car.

"Wait! Sara!" He came around the driver's side, shutting the car door before she could climb inside. "That wasn't what you thought it was."

"Are you serious right now?" Megan exclaimed from the other side of the car.

Harrison glared at her. He did not need the annoying sister getting involved right now. Sara wouldn't look at him. He tipped her chin up, and to his shock, he didn't see sadness in her gaze.

He saw anger. Pure, unmitigated, murderous rage. With her cheeks flushed and her lips thinned, she looked like some avenging angel.

If she wouldn't knee him in the balls for trying it, he'd kiss her right now.

"I don't want to talk to you," she replied in a clipped voice. "You can go out with any woman you want. That's not my problem."

"It is your problem because I wasn't on a date with that woman." At her glare, he explained, "It was a date, but not one I agreed to."

"Seriously?" Megan said again.

He pointed a finger at her. "You, be quiet. You aren't helping. You"—he addressed Sara now—"come with me so we can talk."

When he tried to lead her away, she wrenched her arm away. "Don't pull me around like some ragdoll. I don't want to go with you to hear your excuses."

"And you're being irrational, refusing to listen to me!"

At the word *irrational*, he knew he'd lit a match to the tinder.

"I have every right to be upset." She opened the car door again. "Now, are you going to let me go, or am I going to have to run you over to get home?"

He had a feeling she'd do just that if he let her. Part of him was thankful for her anger: anger meant that she cared. He just needed to get her to listen to him before she unceremoniously ran him over.

"Let me explain, okay? Just give me that. If you aren't satisfied, you can leave," he said in a low voice. "That's all that I'm asking."

She looked like she wanted to refuse, but after a moment, she nodded tightly.

"I'm taking Sara to my place," he said to Megan as he tossed her Sara's car keys.

"Oh, that's fantastic. I'll be sure to stop by to pick her up after she dumps you!" Megan called out as they left to get into Harrison's car.

They were silent on the drive to his house. He wanted to explain, to get her to listen, but he wouldn't do it in the car. She fumed silently, although by the time they arrived, she seemed to have lost some of her initial anger. He led her to the living room and sat down next to her on the couch. Decorated in muted colors of gray and brown, this room was one of Harrison's favorite in the entire house. He'd always found it calming.

He hoped to God that Sara felt the same right now.

Before he could speak, she stood up. "You know what? This is silly. I overreacted. You can date who you want. I've had a long day, and I'm tired, and I probably just need to go home and sleep—"

He tugged on her wrist. "Sit down."

She sat.

"When I got to the restaurant, I had been told that I was meeting my parents for dinner," he began, holding her gaze. "It was only when I was seated with Kayla—the woman you saw me with—that I realized it was a date. Set up by none other than my own mother. Before then, I hadn't even known Kayla existed."

"And so you still had a drink with her?"

"Yes, because it would've been rude not to, and she was a nice woman. We were leaving when you arrived. That's it."

Her cheeks were still flushed, but she wasn't as stiff as when she'd first sat down. "Your mom really set you up on a date without you knowing?"

"If you met my mother, you wouldn't be surprised."

"You had no idea? None at all?"

"None whatsoever. I could strangle my mother if given half the chance right now. She doesn't know when to stop interfering."

Sara narrowed her eyes, assessing him. He felt like she was opening him up from the inside out and peering at every nook and cranny. Having absolutely nothing to hide, he merely raised an eyebrow and waited.

After a few moments of silence, she took a deep breath. "Okay, I believe you."

"Thank God." He said a silent prayer of thanks to any god in the universe listening.

"I have to ask, though: why would your mother try to set you up without even mentioning it to you? That seems...counterintuitive."

"Like I said: if you met my mother, you'd understand," he said wryly. "She refuses to accept that she has no input in any woman I date, and she periodically attempts to set me up with women she finds acceptable."

At that, Sara blanched, and Harrison realized what he'd said. *My mother doesn't think* you *are acceptable.*

"Look, don't worry about my mom," he reassured her. "She's going to do what she's going to do, but she's not going to stop me from making my own damn decisions. Last time I checked, I was a grown man." The last sentence was said in a growl. He didn't need Lisa interfering with his life like this, and especially not if her actions would drive Sara away.

Finally for the first time that evening, Sara smiled. "I have to say, I never expected that a guy like you would need help from his mom to get dates."

He groaned. "God, don't even start. I'm not sure if I'm more pissed off with her or embarrassed by all of this."

"I think I feel badly for the woman who thought she'd be going on a real date the most." Sara scooted closer, and their knees touched. "I know I would've been disappointed to find out that you didn't really want to be on a date with me."

"That would never happen. The first time I'd lay eyes on you, I'd want you."

The moment heated, and Harrison could practically feel the air prickling with energy. Seeing Sara in his living room, her hair tumbling down her back, he couldn't stop the desire pulsing through his entire body. He could taste it on his tongue. Curling an arm around her, he pulled her into his arms.

"Kiss me, Harrison," she pleaded as she gazed up at him. "I need to know that you really want me."

He kissed her, and he let the wave of passion sweep them both away.

9

*S*ara didn't go home with men, and she most definitely didn't go home with men who kissed like consummate seducers. She'd been with a grand total of one man—her ex-husband—and had, for the most part, given up on sex in general.

Now, she realized how wrong she'd been.

Harrison's lips were soft, but he kissed her like he wanted to claim her very soul. She could only hang onto his shoulders and remember to breathe. His stubble scraped at her cheeks, and she loved the reminder of how masculine he was. He made her feel delicate and feminine. She hadn't even known that was something she'd wanted to experience.

He pushed her hair off her shoulder, trailing his fingers through the silken strands. They gazed at each other, and the sheer desire in his eyes made her tremble.

"Will you stay with me?"

She licked her lips. "Yes."

He scooped her up into his arms and carried her upstairs to his bedroom. She felt rather like some kind of fairy princess being swept away by the handsome prince. Until Harrison promptly tossed her onto the bed like a sack of grain. She let out a laugh at the indignity.

"Did you just throw me?" she asked, still laughing.

He climbed over her, caging her in. His forearms bracketed her head, and his pelvis pressed against her.

"Isn't that what you do when you're ravishing a woman? Toss her onto your bed and have your wicked way with her?" He grinned a grin that went straight to her toes.

"I wouldn't know. I'm not in the habit of ravishing anyone."

"That's a damn shame. You deserve to be seduced, ravished... made love to." His eyes darkened at his last words.

Sara could barely keep herself from gasping. *Love, is he talking about love?* Her heart pounded like mad, a bird trapped in the cage of her ribs. She wondered if there was enough oxygen in the room to keep up with her panting breaths.

It didn't help that Harrison was pushing up her blouse, and when she lifted her arms, he pulled off the garment to reveal her silken camisole underneath.

His warmth, his solidity, made her feel safe for the first time in so long. Not only did desire pulse between them, but something that was etching itself onto her very heart. A tattoo that would never fade with time.

He kissed her again, slanting his mouth over hers. She arched against him, and he groaned her name. They kissed like they would never kiss again, like this was the only opportunity they had. It was desperate and intense and beautiful.

"I wanted to kiss you like this the moment I saw you in my office," he admitted as he kissed between her breasts. "I wanted to lay you down and take you right then and there."

She touched his hair. "I'm not sure that's ethical, Dr. Thornton. I'm pretty sure there's some rule about ravishing a patient's mother in the office."

"Mmm, but it's my practice, so don't I make the rules?" He

pushed the straps of her camisole down her arms. "Pretty sure I can do what I want."

"Save me from arrogant men." She sighed, but she was smiling as well.

He smiled up at her, and words she didn't even know she had inside her almost tumbled out. *I need you, I want you, I'm afraid I'm falling in love with you.* Her breath caught, but then the moment broke when Harrison cupped one of her breasts in his hand. He tweaked her nipple through her camisole and bra, but even with the layers of clothing, she felt that touch go straight to her core.

He played with her, making her breasts ache, but she wanted more. Needed more of him. Pushing at his shoulders, she rolled him over and began to unbutton his shirt. He laughed softly.

"Patience," he murmured. "You don't want this to be over too soon."

"Yes, I do, because you're driving me crazy." Sara unbuttoned the last button, now gazing at his chest, his abdomen. He was tanned from the outdoors, and dark hair was scattered across his chest. He was beautiful, she thought with reverence.

As he watched her, she stripped off her camisole. He clenched his jaw as she unhooked her bra. Her breasts bare before him, she couldn't stop the blush crawling up her chest to her cheeks from the look on his face.

She'd never had any man look at her like Harrison did right at this moment.

"You're gorgeous." He tipped her over onto her back. Before she could protest, he took one nipple into his mouth. The sensation curled her toes. She moaned and squirmed and begged as he sucked one nipple and then the other until they were red, swollen berries.

She'd been self-conscious about her body ever since she'd had James, but Harrison made her forget all of that. He didn't notice the faint stretch marks, or that her breasts weren't as perky as they used to be. His mouth roved down her torso, and he stripped her out of her jeans and panties before she even realized he was doing it.

When he parted her legs, though, she froze. Oral sex had never been particularly enjoyable, and she'd never understood why so many women loved it.

He sensed her hesitation. "You okay?"

"Can we skip that? It's not my thing." She gazed up at the ceiling, practically squirming with embarrassment. *Now he's going to think I'm some cold fish. He's probably regretting that he brought me back to his place.*

He kissed her hip. "Is it that you don't like it, or you've never gotten to enjoy it in the first place?"

Oh God, she wanted to die. She wanted to sink below the earth and never come back up. But Harrison wasn't judgmental—simply curious. She chewed her lip.

"I guess the latter," she admitted. "I don't have a lot of experience, really. Which is ironic, considering I was married."

"Let me kiss you. Starting down here." He moved toward her feet, and pressed a kiss to her ankle. "Then if I do anything you don't like, tell me."

"Or I can kick you." She wiggled her toes.

He nipped at her calf. "No kicking, or you're getting put in the corner."

She giggled, but the giggle transformed into a breathy moan when he began to kiss her. Not only kiss her, but touch, stroke, and drink her in. He kissed her feet, which made her laugh, before moving up to her ankles and calves. He told her how beautiful she was, how he was burning with want for her. He traced configurations on her skin; her nerves were on fire, and with every brush of his fingers, it only worsened. He kissed a mole that hid behind her knee, and a freckle on her thigh. By the time he reached her upper thigh, she was vibrating with need.

He parted her legs again. Although she stilled, she forced herself not to panic. He petted her inner thighs, and she relaxed.

"No kicking so far," he commented. He looked up at her with a smile. "All good?"

She swallowed, and to show him just how good it was, she parted her legs further. A slight flush climbed up his cheekbones at the movement. Slowly, infinitesimally, he touched her. Parting her with gentle fingers, he exhaled when her core was revealed to him.

"You're just as pretty here, and so wet and ready for me." He kissed her curls, one finger circling her entrance.

Her breath hitched. She wanted him to go faster because she was pretty sure she would die otherwise. He took his time despite her protests, playing with her, making her wetter with each touch. He knew what she needed without her saying a word, and it only caused her to want him even more. When he pushed a finger inside of her, she clenched around him.

"You're so tight, baby," he muttered.

She grew hotter at his words. Her temperature only rose when he kissed her sex as he stroked his finger inside of her. She made a noise deep in her throat.

"Is this what you want? You want me to kiss you here? Suck your clit until you come?"

"Harrison." She ran her fingers through his hair.

"I can feel you quivering against my tongue. It's the hottest thing I've ever felt." He licked her, and he did it again as his finger continued to move inside of her.

Sara could barely breathe. Her body was like a wire, brimming with electricity, and she was so close to the edge that she wondered if she'd ever come back to herself afterward. Throwing an arm over her eyes, she let herself only feel the sheer exhilaration rushing through her body.

"That's it. Move with me." Harrison circled her clit, and then he sucked it with relentless pressure, drawing out the pleasure until she was mindless from it.

"Oh my God, oh my God," was all she could say until words failed her. With one last touch, she exploded. She screamed, but ended up biting her wrist to stifle the sound. Her entire body shook. Harrison only licked her in light strokes, letting her orgasm last as long as he could.

When she finally came down from the intense high, she was pretty sure she'd never move again. Her bones had melted. Her blood was molten. All she could manage was a moan of protest when he got off the bed.

"Condom," he growled before giving her a hot kiss, and she tasted herself on his lips.

She sat up to watch him rifle inside the bedside drawer. He cursed, slamming the drawer closed before stalking to the bathroom.

She couldn't stop the laugh that bubbled up from her throat. She'd never seen Harrison this out of sorts, and by the sound of the cabinets opening and closing in the bathroom, he wasn't having much luck on the condom front.

"I have an IUD," she said quietly as she approached the bathroom. "I've only been with my ex-husband."

Harrison gazed at her in the mirror, assessing her. "I'm clean."

"Since you're a doctor, I'd hope so."

He didn't waste any time. Pulling her into his arms, he kissed her. She loved the feeling of his skin against hers. The contrast in textures fascinated her. Breaking the kiss, she trailed a hand down his chest before landing on his belt buckle. As he watched, she undid his buckle, unfastening the button at the top of his jeans. He inhaled a breath, and she brushed her fingers above his pelvis.

Hair was sprinkled in a vertical line down his delineated abdomen, and she smiled when she discovered a freckle near his belly button. But her real interest was in the hardness pushing against his fly. She delved below his jeans and boxers to curl her fingers around his cock.

Harrison let her play and stroke him until she felt moisture dotting her palm. He was so hot and hard and big, and the thought of him inside of her, plunging and thrusting, caused her entire body to quiver with need.

When she swirled a thumb over the head of his cock, he swore and pushed her hands away. She almost protested, but he just led her to the bed before stripping out of his clothes completely.

She looked at him in awe. Seeing him completely nude, his cock ruddy and hard, she could hardly believe that this man desired her. Sara Flannigan, once the trailer trash of Fair Haven, had captured the interest of a man like Harrison Thornton.

He crawled over her like before, kissing her. She instantly parted her legs, and his cock was hot against her hip.

"I need you. I need to be inside you."

Harrison touched her sex, and they both made a sound.

"Yes, I need you, too." She arched upward, the tip of his cock now almost inside of her.

She watched as he gritted his teeth, a sheen of sweat on his brow. He slowly plunged inside of her, filling her, until he was lodged to the hilt. Her entire body tingled. She'd never felt this full, this stretched, this *claimed*. He didn't move, though, like he was waiting for her to tell him she was okay.

She dug her nails into his shoulders. "Please," she breathed.

He took that as a yes. Pulling out of her, he thrust inside of her, and she shrieked. When he looked like he was going to stop, she shook her head.

"It's good, so good, don't stop, don't you dare stop." She panted and gasped, like she couldn't find enough air to fill her lungs.

He filled her, over and over again, his strokes unyielding. They never broke eye contact, and somehow, that was almost as erotic as him moving inside of her body. As he moved, she moved with him, and she could feel herself tightening around him.

Tilting her hips up at an angle, she moaned out loud when he brushed against her clit with each thrust. It was just enough friction to send her spiraling all over again. She covered her mouth to stifle her scream, but Harrison pushed her fingers away.

"I want to hear you. Scream for me, Sara."

She let out a breathless laugh, but it came out as a moan. He thrust harder, faster, and as she gazed into his green eyes, she knew without a doubt that she'd fallen in love with him before her orgasm slammed into her like a freight train.

She screamed. He shouted, and they came together. She felt him fill her with his seed, and it was like nothing she'd ever experienced. Closing her eyes, she wondered if she'd died.

If so, she didn't have any regrets.

Sara barely registered Harrison moving up onto the bed, pushing the covers down and then enveloping her in his arms. Her eyelids fluttered. Feeling him press a kiss against her temple, he murmured something, but sleep was already claiming her.

She fell into sleep's embrace, lulled to slumber as she felt Harrison's heartbeat against her cheek.

10

*D*awn peeked through the curtains when Harrison awoke. It only took him a moment to remember everything that had happened the night before, and it caused a wide smile on his face. Sara was still asleep, her breathing easy and slow, and he couldn't help but inhale the scent of her hair. She murmured something but didn't wake up.

After they'd made love, Sara had told him she needed to get home, but he'd persuaded her to stay. She'd texted Ruth to let her know she'd be home before James had to get up for school, although Harrison had seen guilt etch her features.

"He'll never know that you were gone," he'd assured her with a kiss.

"You're right. But that doesn't stop me from feeling like a bad parent."

He kissed her harder, mostly because he didn't want any kind of guilt to stain what had happened between them. Sara had kissed him back, and they'd made love a second time—slow and thorough, until they'd both exhausted themselves.

He squinted at the alarm clock: it was close to five-thirty. Sara needed to be at school by seven. He gently rubbed her shoulder. "Sara," he said in a soft voice. "Wake up."

She groaned and buried her face into the pillow. He grinned and began kissing her neck, her shoulder, her cheek, and she finally turned over with another groan and opened her eyes. He could tell when she remembered everything: her eyes widened, and a slight blush climbed up her face.

"Good morning," he said.

"Good morning. What time is it?"

"Almost five-thirty."

She rubbed her eyes. "I need to get home, but I really don't want to move." She touched his cheek with the backs of her fingers, and he couldn't stop from kissing them.

"Then don't move. Stay with me."

He knew she couldn't stay: he had work, she had work, and her son. Reality called, but that didn't stop him from wishing they could ignore its demand.

"As much as I would love to play hooky with you, I don't think your job or mine would appreciate it." She sat up, and the sheet fell down from her breasts, revealing her nipples.

At his appreciative look, she didn't hide: instead, she let him draw her down for a kiss that turned as hot as lava in just seconds.

"I have to take a shower," she gasped as she pulled away.

He grunted, but he let her go. Grabbing her clothes, Sara went to the bathroom. Harrison listened as she switched on the shower. He lay back in the bed, but he couldn't stop imagining Sara—wet and slick and naked—in the shower.

I have no self-control with her, do I?

He'd never had sex like he'd had last night with Sara Flannigan. It wasn't just that sex had been good—amazing, if he were honest—but it had been tinged with an intensity that both captivated and terrified him. She'd already gotten under his skin and wiggled her way into his heart, and after so short a time. What would happen as time passed? Would his obsession with her only worsen?

He had a feeling he knew exactly the answer to that question.

He leapt from the bed and, entering the bathroom, he pulled the shower curtain away. She gasped. Her eyes took in his aroused state, and he knew she wasn't just flushed from the hot water.

He climbed inside the shower, taking her into his arms. The feeling of her slick breasts rubbing against his chest only made him unbearably hard. His erection bobbed between them.

"I'd make a joke about you being excited to see me, but my brain isn't really working right now." She trailed fingers down his chest, to his belly, swirling soapsuds on his torso.

"Good, because I don't want to think right now." He pushed her hair aside and nipped at her neck. She sighed.

They kissed and touched, their hands as busy as their mouths. They laughed when the shower spray made it difficult to see, and they laughed harder when Sara dropped the soap multiple times. They simultaneously bathed each other and made love, and Harrison couldn't help but love the practicality infused in the eroticism.

"You're gorgeous," she breathed as she kissed down his chest. She twirled a finger around a whorl of chest hair. "I can't get enough of you."

"I'm not sure I'm the gorgeous one here, but I'll take it."

She raised an eyebrow. Moving downward, her mouth hot and insistent, she kneeled before him. His erection only grew, especially as she wrapped her fingers around him. Harrison closed his eyes, but he wanted to watch her. Seeing her on her knees in front of him, licking his cock from root to tip, caused his toes to curl.

She wasn't all that experienced, despite being married. He had a feeling her ex-husband had been a careless lover, and he couldn't stop the pride running through his veins knowing that he'd brought her such pleasure, that he'd shown her things she hadn't experienced before. It was a caveman mentality, but there it was.

Sara cupped his balls as she took his cock into her mouth, swirling her tongue around him. He groaned. He ran his fingers through her hair, although he resisted taking control completely. He wanted her to play—even if they were both late to their jobs that morning. The only thing that mattered in this moment was the pleasure they could give each other.

She sucked him harder, her hand stroking him with each pull of her mouth. Harrison felt his balls draw up, and he knew he was close. So close.

But he didn't want to come like this. Gently pulling her head back, he lifted her up until she was standing again. He kissed away her protest.

"I need to be inside you," he muttered. He moved her so she had her hands flat against the shower wall. He kicked her legs apart. She let out a gasp that turned into a moan when he touched her swollen sex.

She was wet and wanting, and only from sucking his cock. He almost came from just that thought. Positioning himself, he thrust inside her in one stroke. She shuddered, and he wrapped his arms around her to keep her from falling. He took her relentlessly, his cock filling her over and over again. He could hear her saying his name over the sound of the shower.

"Don't stop, Harrison, please don't stop," she begged. "I'm so close."

As if he would ever stop. He thrust harder. He felt her sheath clenching around him the second before she let out a moan that signaled her orgasm. Her body shaking and trembling, he let himself come, flooding her depths, letting himself come inside her until she milked him dry.

Harrison had to hang onto her so she didn't collapse in a heap at his feet. He pulled her to his chest, kissing her as he stroked her breasts. Still inside of her, he didn't move, but instead began to play with her clit with light taps of his finger. Sara trembled. He knew she was on the brink again. His finger rubbed her harder as he pinched her nipple with his other hand. In just a few quick movements, she came again, screaming as he captured the sound with his mouth.

They stumbled from the shower, especially as the hot water turned to cold. Toweling each other off, they finally got dressed.

"Do you want to get coffee or something to eat?" Harrison asked.

Sara glanced at her phone. "If we go really quickly, sure. I'm starving."

"I'd make you something, but I don't think we have time for anything beyond cereal or toast."

"That's okay." She smiled, standing on tiptoe to kiss him. "I'll just consider it an IOU."

He grabbed her ass. "It's a deal."

Luckily, the local coffee place had a short line. Harrison ordered his usual Americano while Sara got a latte, and there was something so domestic about buying coffee together that he couldn't stop from thinking about other small details he wanted to learn about her. What did she eat for breakfast most days? What did she wear around the house? Did she make her bed every morning?

As he drove her home, they stole glances at each other. Yet as the few miles passed, he could sense that Sara was letting her own worries overtake her thoughts. She didn't look at him when he parked the car in front of her house.

"Talk to you later?" he asked.

She hesitated. "Probably." At his look, she made a face. "Sorry, that came out wrong. Don't think I didn't have a great time, because I did. I just need to think. This is really one of those cases of, 'it's not you, it's me.'"

He gave her a wry look. "I'm not sure that's comforting to hear."

"It's the truth." She rubbed her palms against her jeans. "I haven't dated much at all since my divorce, and Kyle was the only man I've ever been with. It's a lot to take in, you know? And I have James to think of, and my job, and—"

"I get it." And he did, even if he didn't want to.

"I'll call you, okay?"

She turned to get out of the car, but he refused to let her leave like this. Gripping her by her elbow, he caught her lips with his in a fierce kiss. It was a kiss of lips and teeth and tongue, and he wanted her to know that she was his and no one else's. She could think about whatever she wanted for as long as she wanted—that didn't mean he was letting her go.

They broke apart. They panted for air until Sara opened the car door.

He watched her go inside her house. Emotions swirled within him, and he could barely identify any of them, they were so tangled together. With Sara Flannigan, he'd go from rapture to frustration in the blink of an eye. Leaning his forehead against the steering wheel, he took a deep breath before driving away.

He didn't need to be at work for another two hours. He considered going home, but it would only remind him of Sara. Without thinking, he drove to Caleb's place, knowing that his brother had the evening shift on Tuesdays and thus wouldn't be working.

He knocked on the front door and waited. Nothing. He knocked again, this time louder. He knew his brother was in there —his patrol car was parked right outside—and for some reason, he needed to talk to somebody. Even if it was just shooting the shit with Caleb.

Finally, Caleb came to the door, rumpled from sleep and looking like he'd cheerfully kick Harrison in the balls. "What the hell?" was his greeting.

"Good morning to you, too. Let's go get something to eat."

Caleb stared at him, looked at the Americano in his hand, and just shook his head. "Give me a minute to put on some actual pants."

They ended up at one of the greasy diners not far from Caleb's place, famous as a place to eat in the middle of the night when people were drunk and hungry. This morning it was mostly empty, although there were a few hung-over people in the corner wincing at every sound. Caleb and Harrison took a booth and ordered various combinations of bacon, eggs, and hash browns, the saltier and the greasier, the better.

Once they'd both eaten and drunk coffee, Caleb pointed a fork at Harrison. "Okay, what was this all about? Because I know you weren't just dying to eat eggs with me on a Tuesday morning."

Harrison took a bite of hash browns. "Can't a guy miss his brother?"

"No, because we see each other all the damn time. If you woke me up on my day off just to eat crappy food with me, I'm going to strangle you."

"It's a wonder you're single with an attitude like that."

Caleb just waited.

Harrison didn't know if he wanted to talk about Sara. He'd wanted company, and a distraction, but he had a distinct feeling he'd know what Caleb would say if he told him: *the Flannigans are trouble. You're an idiot. What are you doing?*

Something to that effect.

But despite his surliness, Caleb wasn't the type to let something lie. Sighing, he set his fork down and gave Harrison a searching look. "You were with her last night, weren't you?"

He stared at his plate. If he didn't know better, he was on the edge of blushing like a schoolgirl.

"Jesus Christ, I'm right, aren't I? And now you're all broken up about it because she probably told you it wasn't going to happen again, right?"

Harrison blinked at his younger brother. "Now you're freaking me out."

"The Flannigan women are fairly predictable."

"What the hell does that mean?"

Realizing he'd said too much, Caleb decided to drink his coffee. And drink it. And drink some more.

"You know what, I don't want to know," Harrison said. "You and Megan Flannigan will kill each other one day, and we'll all be thankful because we won't have to listen to you fight as you try to ignore that you want to rip each other's clothes off."

Caleb opened his mouth. Then closed it.

"The night we had together..." Harrison grunted. "It was unbelievable. And now she tells me she needs to 'think things over.'"

"What does that even mean? Why do women say shit like that?"

"If I knew, I'd be a billionaire."

They fell silent. Caleb finally asked, "You really like her, don't you?"

"Yeah, I do."

Harrison didn't know if he could classify it as *liking* at this point: liking was too passive, too simple. This was anything but simple. She'd infected his blood, taken over his thoughts, made his life difficult. Sara Flannigan had burst into his life, and without so much as a glance, she'd captured him and chained him to the metaphorical wall.

It wasn't, perhaps, the most positive metaphor, but at the moment, his thoughts weren't all that positive to begin with.

"Then if you really like her, don't let her go," Caleb said. "Because we both know you'd regret it."

"Did I tell you that she saw me on a date Mom had set up?"

"What? Wait, what did Mom do?"

Harrison regaled his brother with the story, which caused Caleb to swear and laugh at equal turns. "When she saw us together, she was pissed. She would barely let me get in an explanation."

"Good. It means she got jealous. If she's jealous, she cares."

"You sound like a shrink."

"I'm a cop. We're basically shrinks with a gun."

They paid the bill, and Harrison walked back to Caleb's place. The brothers didn't talk on the way there, although Harrison felt better than he had an hour ago. *If she's jealous, she cares.* Then why did she need to think things over now?

"Wait and call her later," Caleb advised. "Let her think, but don't let her think too long. And if all else fails, toss her over your shoulder and abduct her."

"I thought you were a cop."

Caleb smiled. "I'm not on duty right now. See you later, lover boy."

11

*W*hen her classroom computer refused to boot up, Sara sighed. "Everyone, please take out your reading assignment and begin that while I try to get the computer sorted out."

Her third graders made a few murmurs, but otherwise obediently delved into their desks and pulled out the reading material she'd originally assigned as homework. When she saw that everyone was reading—or at least pretending to read—she called the front office.

"Hey, Linda, can you send someone to my classroom to help me with my computer? It refuses to turn on. And yes, it is plugged in. Okay. Thanks."

She glanced at the clock. She really hated when she got off schedule, but you couldn't plan with technology. It either worked, or it didn't. She should've made certain to have a back-up plan in case her computer went on the fritz, but she needed it to show a video for a health lesson. Tapping her fingers against her desk, Sara was about to call Linda again when someone knocked on the classroom door.

"It's open!" Madison, one of her students, yelled.

Sara shushed the class as they erupted into laughter. "Reading. Now."

Opening the door, she was still looking at her class when she heard the voice of the AV guy drawl, "Hello."

She froze. Turning, she saw that the AV guy was none other than Devin Yates, who'd called her a slut at the Fainting Goat only weeks ago. Who Harrison had taken outside and punched.

She stared at him, while he just smirked. Why in God's name was he *here*? In her school?

"Just got hired," he explained. "Can I come in?" His tone suggested that it wasn't a question, but more of a dare, like he knew she wanted to tell him no.

She wanted to slam the door in his face, but if she made a scene, her class would never recover. Swallowing, she opened the door to allow Devin inside.

"Linda said your computer isn't working?" He walked to the offending device and kneeled down beside it. An old desktop model, it needed to be upgraded, but Sara hadn't had the time to put in the request.

"That's right. It won't turn on."

Devin began to work, and Sara let out a silent breath. *Maybe he was too drunk to remember. Maybe he feels badly. Maybe the sky is yellow and pigs do fly.*

Sara walked through the rows of desks, making certain her students continued to read silently. She caught Alison Decker passing a note to Cassie Andrews, and Sara snagged the note with a whispered, "This is your first warning," to both girls. She pocketed the note. Although most of her kids had phones and texted regularly, no phones were allowed at their desks for obvious reasons. Thus, students still tried to pass the occasional paper note during class, which Sara found both frustrating and amusing at the same time. What in the world did eight and nine-year-olds have to gossip about? Lots of things, she'd discovered as her collection of notes only increased with every passing day.

"Looks like your power cord was chewed through," Devin said. He held it up. "I'll get you another one."

After he left, Madison stage-whispered to Sara, "Are there *rats* in here, Ms. Flannigan?"

"I heard one in the wall last week," Reagan said. A big, blond boy who loved anything creepy crawly, Reagan was always looking for a way to freak out the girls in his class.

"I doubt you heard a rat, Reagan. Madison, I'll be sure to have one of the janitors put down traps, just in case. If it's anything, it's tiny mice chewing on the cords."

"You should get a cat, then. My cat hunts mice really good," Madison said.

"Get back to your reading, you two."

Devin returned and in a few minutes, had Sara's computer up and running.

"Ms. Flannigan, can I show you something?" Devin asked, gesturing to her.

She hesitated, but she approached him, wariness in every step. She kneeled next to him. They were now half-hidden by the desk and the computer.

"What did you want to show me?"

He turned his face toward her, and she realized he was only inches away. "I hope there are no hard feelings," he said in a low voice. "You know, with what happened."

"I don't—"

"Because I'm trying to turn over a new leaf. Get my life together." He leaned closer toward her. "You're a beautiful woman, you know that, right?" He touched her hand.

She stood up, so abruptly that Devin almost fell over. "Thank you for showing me that," she said loudly. "Do you need anything else? Otherwise I need to return to teaching."

He stood slowly, his expression darkening. She waited for him to say something, but he just shook his head before exiting the classroom.

She told her students to put their reading away so they could return to the planned lesson, her hands behind her back to hide their shaking.

∽

SARA SAT with Heath and Kelly, one of the PE teachers and the girls' basketball coach, while at lunch. They usually ate in the teacher's lounge, which consisted of a handful of tables and chairs, two vending machines, and a sink that inevitably filled with dirty dishes that no one washed.

Heath and Kelly chatted, mostly about the upcoming parent-teacher conferences and various teacher gossip. Kelly collected gossip like a bird collected twigs for a nest. Sara didn't know how Kelly managed to find all of this information, but if anyone knew something, it would be her.

"So Phyllis apparently parked in Principal Anderson's spot and got in big trouble for it," Kelly said before she took a bite of her kale salad, as part of her perpetual dieting regime. Kelly had more muscles than any woman Sara had ever met, and she worked out with a diligence that Olympic athletes would envy. "Phyllis said she wasn't paying attention, but everybody knows that spot is his. Apparently she got reprimanded and ended up crying in her office."

"How do you know this again?" Heath asked with a wry smile. "And anyway, I've definitely seen Linda park in that same spot on the days Principal Anderson isn't here."

"She would, since she handles his calendar."

Sara stared at her own salad, her stomach in knots. Ever since Devin had appeared in her classroom that morning, she could barely concentrate on teaching. It had been a struggle all morning, and when the lunch bell had rung, she'd heard it with immense relief.

She had intended to talk to Principal Anderson about Devin's hiring, but Kelly had already filled her in on how he'd gotten hired in the first place. Devin's mother was good friends with Principal Anderson's own wife Teresa, and they'd done him a favor by hiring him as an AV tech. And with a sinking realization, Sara had discovered that Teresa Anderson was good friends with none other than Lisa Thornton—Harrison's mother.

Harrison. Her heart hurt when she thought of him. He'd be furious when he found out about Devin being hired, and he'd probably wring Devin's neck if Sara told him about his behavior toward her. But if Sara filed a complaint, would she be believed? She remembered how she'd been treated all those years ago in high school, when she'd been accused of sleeping with multiple members of the football team. She'd gone to the principal then, but her complaint had been brushed aside. "Don't let the bullies get to you," had been his advice. "These things happen."

Given the complicated relationships in this instance, Sara had a distinct impression that she'd only make things worse if she said anything.

"Hey, Sara, are you okay?" Kelly asked.

Sara looked up to see both Kelly and Heath staring at her.

"You were frowning pretty fiercely at that salad," Heath remarked.

She laughed, although it sounded brittle to her ears. "No, sorry, I'm fine. I think I'm going to take a walk before class starts again, though. See you guys later?"

She packed up her lunch, which she'd barely touched, and placed it in the fridge for tomorrow. Heath gave her a concerned look, and Kelly looked like she wanted to demand answers. Sara hurried out of the school until she reached the parking lot, which was mostly deserted. The temperature had dropped, and she wished she'd worn her coat, but it was too late to go back. Besides, the cold would help clear her head.

She walked to the edge of the baseball diamond, which was perched below a tall hill that overlooked Fair Haven's downtown. She stood silently and let her thoughts dissipate. Devin Yates wouldn't ruin her job—not like he'd ruined her life in high school. She wasn't that same young girl anymore.

I wish Harrison were here, she thought, and her heart twisted in her chest.

She checked the time and made her way back to the school. As she approached, she saw a figure in her peripheral vision.

She stilled, convinced that Devin had followed her outside.

But to her relief, it was one of the other teachers, and he gave her a friendly wave as he returned inside the school.

Her heart pounding, she closed her eyes and took a deep breath. *He wasn't following you. You're just freaking yourself out for no reason.*

She took one last deep breath before going back inside.

"OPEN WIDE FOR me and say 'aaaah.' Atta boy." Harrison looked inside James's mouth before setting the tongue depressor aside. "Everything looks good. I won't need to see you again for another six months."

James kicked his feet, already bored with the appointment they'd scheduled after school on Thursday. Sara let out a sigh of relief: although Harrison had assured her multiple times that James was fine, it was still something else entirely to hear it confirmed once again. She couldn't stop herself from sitting on the table with James and putting an arm around him. He protested, but she just squeezed him tighter, ruffling his hair.

"Mom, let me go. Are you crying? Why are you crying? I'm okay now. Or is Dr. Thornton lying?" James narrowed his eyes.

Sara laughed as she brushed stray tears away. "No, he's not lying. I'm just happy."

"Oh." James was nonplussed. He looked over at Harrison. "She does that sometimes, you know."

"Cries?" Harrison asked.

"Cries, but she says she's happy. I don't get it, though. I only cry when I'm sad."

Harrison nodded solemnly, although Sara could see the twinkle in his eye. "It's an adult thing. You'll understand when you're older."

James shrugged.

Sara hadn't seen Harrison since she'd spent the night at his house two weeks ago, although they'd called and texted every day. He'd been busy with work, and she'd been similarly busy with parent-teacher conferences and caring for James, especially when Ruth had fallen ill with the flu and hadn't been able to babysit, while Megan had had to work longer hours at the bakery now that Daria was on maternity leave. As far as Sara knew, Jubilee hadn't yet applied for the position at the Rise and Shine.

Sara had hated not seeing Harrison, but the logical part of her mind had felt that the brief separation had been necessary. She hadn't lied when she'd told him that she needed to think. She needed to grapple with the possibility that her life would be changing if she were to continue with this relationship, and if she wanted that change to happen.

Mostly, though, she was overly aware of the gulf between them with every passing day. Harrison Thornton, the eligible bachelor, eldest of the Thornton clan, renowned physician, was not the type of man who would be interested in a woman like Sara Flannigan. It didn't help that Devin continued to work at the school, and although Sara only saw him occasionally, he never failed to sneer at her or make certain she felt unwelcome there. He never failed to remind her of the black spot on her past.

Harrison opened the door of his office and stepped out for a moment. She heard him speak to one of his nurses. "Jackie, can you take James up to the front so I can speak with Sara for a moment?"

Jackie smiled at James when she entered the room. "How about we go have some fun for a second? I brought some new coloring books you can color."

James shrugged again, but he went with Jackie without protest. After Harrison closed the door, Sara found it difficult to look him in the eye. She wasn't embarrassed by what had happened between them, but being alone with him inevitably made her on edge. It was like an energy she'd never before experienced, making it difficult to keep her thoughts straight.

"I'm sorry we haven't been able to get together," he said in a quiet voice. "I know you're not here to talk to me about this, but I have a feeling we won't have a chance anytime soon."

She looked up, and seeing his sincere gaze was almost too much. She wanted to launch herself into his arms, feel his warmth. Tell him all of her fears and doubts and insecurities.

"I've been busy, too. That's life, I guess."

"I want to take you out on Saturday. Are you free?"

She hesitated, and he caught the hesitation. Frowning, he took her hand. "Are you alright? You seem distracted today."

"I've just been busy," she hedged, getting off the table. "I don't know if I'll have a babysitter for Saturday. I'll let you know."

"Your mom isn't available?"

Sara bit her lip. Ruth was better now and wouldn't object to babysitting if asked, but for some reason, Sara couldn't commit right now. *He's a Thornton, you're a Flannigan.* She saw Devin's sneering face in her vision, remembered the whispers when she'd been in high school.

"I'll let you know. I should get James home."

She collected her son at the front, although he was busy coloring in a superhero coloring book and complained when she told him he had to leave it behind.

"He can have it," Jackie said. "I have plenty more."

"Yay!" James crowed.

Sara said, "What do you say?"

"Thank you!"

Sara gathered their things, but not before Harrison stepped into the front room, a frown etching his features. She knew he wanted to talk further. Using James like a shield—she winced inwardly at her cowardice—she gave them all a hasty goodbye.

HARRISON RUBBED his forehead as he watched Sara and James leave without a look back. Stuffing his hands into his doctor's coat, he wondered for the millionth time what had gone wrong so quickly. *Did we move too fast?* he thought, frustrated by her reticence and mixed signals.

Their night together had been so amazing, and she'd been so receptive and seemingly happy that he had no idea what had changed. He wanted to chase after her and demand answers, but he had his next patient coming within the hour. He had a feeling demanding answers would only cause her to clam up even more.

"I'm not one to pry—" Jackie began as they walked down the hallway together.

Harrison just looked at her.

"Okay, yes I am. But I'm thinking you need to talk to her."

He blew out a breath, laughing a little. "I figured that one out myself, but she won't talk to me. Not really. Except that she responds to all of my texts and phone calls, and she acts interested. Then today, she runs away from me like I've threatened her dog."

Jackie made a noise in her throat. "If you want my advice..."

"Do I have a choice?"

"No, you don't." She pointed at him with her pen. "That woman doesn't know what she wants, and I would bet you my entire bank account—which isn't much, considering I've yet to get a raise this year, you know—that she's scared as hell and doesn't know what to think or feel."

"Jackie, I give you a raise every year."

"Don't change the subject. You need to make Sara feel like she's safe. She's had a life where she's never really felt safe. You get me? She needs that kind of security."

He frowned. "So what should I do? Tell her I'll take care of her? I've already shown her that I'll punch a guy to defend her honor," he added in a sardonic tone.

"It's not about that..." She shook her head. "Women have to know if they let themselves be vulnerable that it's safe to do so, and Sara probably needs more safety than most women. She's gone through a lot."

Harrison stared out the window that overlooked the parking lot. He could just make out Sara and James getting into the car.

"Maybe she just doesn't want this," he murmured. "Or me, for that matter."

Jackie rolled her eyes. "Now you're getting on my nerves. She wants you, you want her, but it's not that simple. My advice? Be patient, but direct."

Sara drove off, and Harrison considered Jackie's words. Was she just scared? It would make sense, given her history with her ex-husband, and then battling James's cancer. She'd seen how difficult life could be at an early age.

I want to give her the happiness she deserves, he thought. *Even if she keeps trying to run from me.*

It was that promise to himself that propelled him through the rest of the day.

12

*L*isa Thornton was, in a word, sulking. Harrison had chewed her out after the disaster with Kayla two weeks ago, telling her in no uncertain words that she was never to try to set him up on a date again. He'd been harsher with his mother than he'd actually intended, but remembering Sara's face when she'd thought he'd been two-timing her had sealed that particular coffin.

Now during the monthly family dinner, Lisa refused to give Harrison any of her attention beyond a passing remark or two. Caleb looked amused, while Jubilee looked like she wanted everyone to get along. Dave merely advised his eldest son to give his mother time to calm down. Lisa had a tendency to sulk longer than most people, but she would, in time, get over it.

Or so Harrison told himself when Lisa ignored his request for her to pass the salt for a third time.

"Here." Caleb reached over, grabbed the salt, and handed it to Harrison.

Lisa gave them both a peeved look. She hated when people reached across the dinner table.

Jubilee bit her lip. Sitting next to Harrison, she remained

mostly quiet. He knew his younger sister hated conflict, especially amongst her family members. Perhaps that was why the Thorntons so often resorted to silence when angry: any outward displays of emotion with each other only upset Jubilee, who had been cossetted due to her illness. No one wanted to upset Jubilee; it was a rule that had never completely gone away.

The Thorntons had grown up in the same house in which they ate dinner tonight. The house sat in the hills of Fair Haven, overlooking the lake. A palatial estate, it housed a bedroom for each child, plus a number of guest rooms. The dining room was newly decorated in soft colors, with nothing brighter than a muted green to be seen. A chandelier hung overhead, somehow still tasteful and demure despite its sparkling appearance. The china they ate on was one of many sets that Lisa owned: she loved to collect entire collections of china—not just the plates and cups, but the gravy boats, serving platters, and teapots, too, even if they were rarely used.

As a kid, Harrison hadn't realized the immensity of his family's fortune and privilege. He'd assumed everyone lived in a house like this. It wasn't until he was older that he discovered most people didn't enjoy prosperity like this, although it was only recently that he found himself almost embarrassed by all of it. Or perhaps he'd become overly aware of how he'd lived compared to Sara, whose family had struggled in poverty for years, especially with Ruth's alcoholism. Sara had admitted to him that she still had to restrain herself from hoarding food most days out of sheer habit. As a kid, there were too many times to count when she and Megan didn't know where their next meals would come from. While Harrison had never gone a day hungry or cold or even uncomfortable.

He gazed at the shining crystal of his wine glass, and for a brief moment, he hated everything his family stood for.

Silence reigned at the table. It was Jubilee who broke the awkward silence.

"I got a job," she said to no one in particular. "Finally." Although she'd moved out of the family home, she'd struggled to find a job, mostly due to her lack of work experience.

"Where are you going to work, Jubi?" Caleb asked.

She smiled. "At the Rise and Shine."

Caleb choked on his bite of steak; Harrison slapped him on the back, while their parents looked on in confusion. They knew that Caleb had arrested Megan Flannigan years ago, but nothing beyond that.

"That's great," Harrison said, truly happy that his suggestion to Jubilee had worked out. "When do you start?"

"This Saturday. Megan told me she's going crazy since Daria went on maternity leave, and she needs someone ASAP."

"So does that mean you're going to make me cinnamon rolls?" Caleb asked after he'd chugged down some water.

"If you pay for them, sure," Jubilee answered. "I do nothing for free, you know."

"A bakery, though? Are you sure you're up for that?" Lisa clucked her tongue. "You get so tired, sweetheart. Bakeries are a lot of work. And remember the last time you tried to make a cake?"

Jubilee blushed scarlet. "I can learn. And Megan is going to do the baking. I'm helping her, with the register, cleaning, that kind of stuff."

"Good for you," Dave offered, nodding in approval. "I'm glad to see you take this step. Make sure you're always on time and do what you're told."

Jubilee gave Harrison a *Help me* look. He just smiled. Caleb grunted, looking like he'd love to say something sarcastic.

"Caleb can tell you all about Megan Flannigan," Harrison said. He grinned wider at Caleb's dirty look. "They're great friends, aren't you?"

"Shut up, Harrison," Caleb growled.

"Really? Since when? And why do you look like you'd rather eat your arm than talk about her?" Jubilee frowned.

"Because I would rather eat any one of my body parts than talk about this," Caleb retorted.

"Why are we talking about something like this?" Lisa scrunched up her nose. "Dave, what is wrong with your children?"

"They're only my children when they're cannibals, I suppose," Dave remarked.

The conversation devolved from there. Caleb refused to answer Jubilee's questions about Megan, while Lisa tried to talk to Harrison about going on another date with a woman she'd met at the Fair Haven country club. "She's an ER physician, and is recently divorced. No children, however. Very pretty, although perhaps a little too tall."

"I'm sure she's a lovely person. Still not interested."

"Why are you so stubborn? You know I want you to be happy. You should be married by now. When will I have grandchildren? By the time any of you get around to it, I'll be six feet under." Lisa brushed away what Harrison thought was an imaginary tear.

"Darling, we both know I'll die far before you will," Dave said in a soothing voice. "And you can't force our kids to date anyone they don't want to date."

Lisa sniffed. "That being said, they should at least take my advice."

"Once again, I know you mean well, but you're wasting your time and any woman's time as well." Harrison set down his fork. "I'm dating Sara Flannigan, if you must know."

The table fell silent again. Everyone knew he was seeing Sara, but to his family, it hadn't been made official. Jubilee raised her eyebrows, while Caleb just waited for their mother's blow-up. But before Lisa could say a word, Dave slapped Harrison on the shoulder. "Great news, son. Now, can we eat some dessert already?

Because I've been dreaming about that pie your mother made since yesterday."

Lisa pursed her lips. Harrison silently thanked his father for the reprieve.

After dessert, the family retired to the sitting room, like they were in some kind of Victorian novel. Harrison couldn't help the wash of disdain when took in the expensive furnishings that filled the room.

He knew he was being unfair to his family. He'd lived a charmed life, and for that, he was immensely grateful. Yet he couldn't stop thinking of Sara as a child, and how she'd suffered when he'd lived in a house like this.

Lisa sat down next to Harrison. He expected another grilling, but she seemed to have decided to accept his decision—for now.

"You know I want the best for you and all of your siblings," she said quietly. She patted his knee like she did when she was being conciliatory. "I know how difficult it can be to go against people's expectations. The whispers, the rumors, the glances." Her lips thinned, her gaze faraway.

Lisa had faced her own difficulties when she'd gone against convention to marry David Thornton, the illustrious heir to the Thornton family fortune. Harrison knew she wanted her own children to avoid the same heartbreak that had resulted.

He squeezed her hand. "I know, Mom."

"You don't know, though. You don't know what it was like." She squeezed his hand harder. "Right after your father and I married, no one would let us buy a house. We had to rent a tiny apartment at the outskirts of town because the landlord was a family friend of my parents. I couldn't go to the grocery store in town because people wouldn't look at me, or they'd make snide comments about how I'd clearly trapped your father into marrying him."

Harrison stayed silent. He'd never heard this much detail about his parents' early life together. His mother, so strong and commanding, seemed bent over with the memories at this moment. He just held her hand, hoping he could understand this woman who had confounded him his entire life.

"I'm not saying this to make you feel sorry for me. I'm saying this because I *know*. I know what will happen if you get involved with Sara Flannigan. Your life will be hard, Harrison. You will face things you never expected. I can't bear to think of you shouldering that burden."

"Mom, your marriage was decades ago. Times have changed." He rubbed her fingers.

She shook her head. "Not that much. Not here."

He didn't know what to say to that. Was she right? Would they face harassment from people like Devin for years to come? The thought of Sara facing that kind of pain made him both depressed and angry. He'd fight for her no matter what happened, damn anyone who thought otherwise.

"Just, promise me you won't do anything hasty," Lisa implored. "Please."

Harrison just nodded. She rose and went to Dave's side, leaving Harrison alone for the time being.

The evening passed slowly, Harrison only tuning into various conversations a handful of times. As he considered going home, he heard Lisa say, "He got a job at the elementary school. Teresa pulled a favor. He's had a hard time of it, you know, but he says he's sober now."

Harrison stilled at her words. "Who got a job, Mom?"

Lisa turned toward him. "Devin Yates. You know, Holly Yates's son? He needed a job, and Teresa pulled some strings down at the school."

Harrison didn't hear what else his mother had to say. His only thoughts were that Devin was at Sara's school, and she hadn't told him. Did she know Devin had been hired there? It was a small enough school, so the odds were likely. Fear and rage swirled inside of him at the thought that Devin could hurt Sara again.

"You okay?" Caleb asked in a low voice.

Harrison stood. "I need to go home. I'll see you all later."

His parents protested, and Jubilee tried to get him to stay, but he was insistent. After making his goodbyes, he went out to his car, Caleb following.

"Devin Yates is working at Sara's school," Harrison growled when Caleb was about to ask him what was wrong a second time. "I'll kill him."

Caleb knew what had happened, although few other people did. Harrison imagined that Devin had been too humiliated to let the story spread.

Caleb's eyes widened. "Well, shit."

"Yeah. Exactly. And don't tell me that murder is illegal because you're a cop."

Caleb just shrugged. "Doesn't mean I won't help you kill him. I'm not on duty now, anyway."

Harrison leaned against his car. Caleb didn't say anything as Harrison tried to calm himself. He had always appreciated that his younger brother knew when to stay silent.

"You going to go see Sara?" Caleb asked quietly.

"Yeah. I need to talk to her. Tell Mom and Dad sorry for me?"

"Sure, but you owe me. And don't do anything I wouldn't do."

Harrison just laughed darkly as he got into his car.

SARA HAD JUST CLOSED James's bedroom door for the night when she heard the knock. Frowning, she went to the front door, but she didn't open the door. A second knock, although this time it was a little louder.

"Can I help you...?" Sara opened the door. She blinked when

she realized that Harrison Thornton was standing in front of her, looking both handsome and agitated at the same time. "What are you doing here? Is everything all right?"

"I wanted to ask you that same question. Can I come in?"

She hesitated, but only because she didn't want to wake James. "I just put James to bed, so we'll have to be quiet. If he hears your voice, he'll never fall asleep."

That got a smile from him. She ushered him to the living room, where she'd been reading a magazine and sipping tea. "Can I get you anything?"

He shook his head. "I'm fine. I came the second I heard." At her confused look, he added, "About Devin being hired at the school."

She paled.

"Sara, has he said anything to you? Dammit, if he's done something else, I'll wring his scrawny neck—"

She shushed him. "It's fine. I've only seen him a handful of times." She considered telling him about what Devin had said when he came to fix her computer, but she decided not to. Why upset Harrison further?

Harrison, though, sensed she wasn't telling the full truth. Narrowing his eyes at her, he asked again, "Has he said anything to you? You can tell me, you know."

"And if I do? What will you do? Go down to the school and punch him?" She lowered her voice. "Look, I can take care of myself. I would've filed a complaint, but there's no point. I'm better off keeping my head down and continuing to work."

"Why can't you file a complaint? That man harassed you! He has no business working at that school."

"Why do you think? He's friends with the principal's wife, and the principal's wife is friends with *your* mother." The words tumbled from her lips before she could catch them.

Harrison went still. His lips thin, he asked in a strangled voice, "What does my mom have to do with any of this?"

"Look, I'm tired. You don't have to worry about Devin."

"Sara, look at me."

She pursed her lips and continued to stare at her abandoned mug of tea.

"What does my mom have to do with this?" His voice was tight.

"She—and everyone she considers friends—has everything to do with this." He flinched at her words, but Sara was too tired to censor herself. "The Thorntons' word is law in Fair Haven. You know that; don't act like you don't. If I made a complaint about Devin, it would get back to Teresa Anderson and, yes, your mom, and they would counter that I was just making trouble for a nice guy like Devin Yates."

"How can you say that about them? You don't even know my mother!"

She rubbed her temples. "I don't want to insult your mom. I don't. But there's history here—"

"Like what?"

"I'm never going to be accepted by people like your mom! You know that. I know you know that. This all goes hand in hand with that. Don't act naïve, Harrison."

He clenched his jaw. "It's not naïve to say that, once again, you don't know my mother. Even if she doesn't approve of you, she wouldn't agree that you deserve to be *harassed*."

Sara sighed. "Drop it, okay? This is only going to end badly. You have a right to defend your mom. I get it. Just don't try to intervene on my behalf when you don't understand the full story."

"How can I understand when you won't tell me the full story?"

She hesitated. She wanted to tell him what had happened back in high school—after he'd already left for college—but then she imagined his pity. Or worse—the judgment. What if he didn't believe her either? What if he was just like her old principal, saying she needed to get over it, and where there's smoke, there's fire?

"You should go," was all she said as she rose from the couch. "I have to get up for work tomorrow, as I'm sure you do, too."

Harrison stood, but he didn't move toward the front door. Instead, he stared down at her, searching her face. Like she were a puzzle he just couldn't figure out.

"I can't protect you if you don't let me in," he said softly. "I don't get why you won't tell me the truth."

"I'm not lying to you." *I'm just not telling you everything.*

"Fine, you're evading my questions. There's little difference."

She wished she could confide in him about everything, that she had the courage to speak, but her tongue felt like it was tied in knots. Syllables stymied in her throat. Gazing up at him, she wished she could communicate to him with just a breath or a look.

He brushed gentle fingers along her jaw. Memories of their night together flooded her, and her body instantly heated. Seemingly sensing the trajectory of her thoughts, his own gaze darkened.

"Sara." His voice was little more than a growl.

She didn't want words. She wanted sensation. Grasping his chin, she pulled him down for a kiss.

It only took a second for him to kiss her back and to take over the kiss. He hugged her so tightly the breath whooshed from her lungs, and his tongue slicked inside her mouth, dominating her completely. She mewled, she moaned, she tasted him, and it was like a heady elixir. As his lips moved desperately across her own, she wished with everything inside her heart that this moment would never end.

"Go out with me again," he said, after what felt like hours later.

She trembled, and for once, she listened to her heart instead of to her brain.

She whispered, "Yes."

13

"*I*t's beautiful," Sara said in awe as she gazed out onto the lake. Wearing a wide-brim straw hat and sunglasses over a sundress, she looked springy and beautiful, her hair loose around her shoulders. Harrison steered the sailboat with a light touch, no particular destination in mind for the afternoon's outing. With the shining sun and sparkling lake, it was like some kind of paradise.

Or maybe it was the woman smiling up at him that made it a paradise. Sara seemed relaxed for once, and she looked younger as a result. It only made Harrison want her even more than usual. Did she not realize how beautiful she was when she smiled?

A number of other people were on the lake today, although it was still fairly deserted, given the time of year. Boating season wouldn't start for another few months, but Harrison liked to take advantage of any break in the rainy spring weather if he could. When the sun had risen this morning and promised to stay shining, he'd asked Sara if she'd like to go out on the lake for their date.

"I love it out here," she murmured. "I missed this when I lived in Seattle."

"There are no lakes in Seattle?" Harrison teased.

She elbowed him lightly. "No real opportunity to be on one. Besides, Fair Haven has its own kind of beauty. I like that it's such a small town. It has a peacefulness that you don't get in a bigger city."

"Why did you move away?" He thought he knew the answer, but for some reason, he wanted to hear it for himself.

Sara rubbed her arms. "A few reasons. I got pregnant with James, and Kyle and I were newly married. And I wanted to get away from some things." She shrugged. "Unfortunately, you can never really run from your problems. They'll always catch up with you again."

"But your mom is sober now, right? She's doing better?"

"She is. She's been sober a year, and she's worked hard on being an actual parent. Sometimes I feel like it's too little, too late, but she's also the reason I returned here. I wanted to help her get back on her feet."

Harrison felt his admiration for her grow. She'd given up her life in Seattle to move in with her mom, even after all of the years when Ruth Flannigan had been less than a stellar parent. He didn't know if he had the strength to do something like that. Something else niggled at him, though: was there another a reason why Sara had wanted to leave Fair Haven, something having to do with Devin Yates?

"Sara," he said after he put up the sail, letting the boat rest in the water, "is there another reason why you left?"

"What do you mean?"

He considered her. He didn't want to push her too hard, but if they were dating, he should know her history, especially with Devin working at her school now.

"With Devin, and what he said to you. That couldn't have been something out of the blue. What happened?"

She turned away, and he wondered if she was going to answer

him. Inhaling deeply, the words tumbled from her mouth. "In high school, there were rumors...about me."

His gut clenched. "What kind of rumors?"

"Rumors that I was easy, I guess. That I'd slept with the entire football team, or a bunch of guys on it, depending on who you asked." She stared down at her feet. "Devin was one of the main instigators of that rumor, especially after I rejected him when he tried to get me to go out with him. The rumors and whispers were endless. I got harassed by so many guys, who thought I was an easy lay. I got gross notes in my locker, stuffed into my backpack. I'm only grateful that this was before social media was a thing, otherwise it would've a million times worse."

Rage roared through Harrison, listening to Sara recount this story in a toneless voice. He'd known Devin was scum, but this? Red washed over his vision, and it took him a moment to find his voice.

"Jesus Christ, Sara, I'm sorry. I'm sorry I wasn't there to stop it. I didn't know." He swore underneath his breath.

"You didn't know. How could you? You'd already left for college, and we didn't really know each other back then."

"That doesn't make me feel less guilty. I can't imagine the hell that you went through. No wonder you left as soon as you graduated."

She fiddled with her hair. "So you believe me?"

"Believe you?"

"You don't think I really was sleeping around like everyone else thought I was?"

At that, he could only shake his head in disbelief. "Even if you did sleep with the entire *school*, you didn't deserve to be treated like you did."

He took her into his arms, although she was stiff in his embrace. Like she couldn't believe he still wanted to touch her.

After a moment, she softened, and she wrapped her arms around him.

"I'll kill him, you know," he said in a low voice. "I'll punch him until he begs for forgiveness, the disgusting little weasel."

"Part of me would like you to do just that, but he'll get his punishment. Karma and all that."

Her face tilted toward him, but he wanted to see her eyes. He took off her sunglasses to see that she had unshed tears in her eyes.

"You're the most amazing woman I've ever met."

The tears only increased, but she shook her head. "I'm not anything special. I'm just trying to get through life."

"No, you are. You're brave, loyal, and kind. You don't let life get you down. You keep fighting. There's so much to admire about you."

"And what about you? You're curing kids with cancer. You love your family, and you're thoughtful and sweet and—"

"Sweet? That's going a little too far," he teased.

She poked him. "*Sweet* and devastatingly handsome. How about that?"

"I'll take it." He held her close, and he couldn't resist the temptation of her lips. Kissing her, he tasted her own innate sweetness on his tongue. Her breasts pressed against his chest. He trailed his hands down her back to squeeze her ass.

The kiss heated up. He kissed down her throat, pale and silky, and he felt her pulse fluttering against his tongue. He needed her with an ache that would never abate. Taking her by the hand, he sat down on a nearby seat and pulled her onto his lap. The skirt of her dress billowed around them, and the brim of her hat shaded them both from the sun.

He needed to touch every inch of her skin. But they weren't completely hidden from view from the other boats, so he had to content himself with touching underneath her dress. That somehow made things even more erotic: the small of her back, the dip of her cleavage, the soft skin of her inner thighs. He reveled in the satin texture of her skin, the brush of downy hairs. Discovering a mole above her belly button.

He couldn't stop himself from delving below, wanting to touch the very heart of her. She didn't protest—instead, she pushed into his hand, wordlessly begging. Her curls were already moist, and when he parted her, he found her wet and wanting.

"Harrison," she breathed. "Can we do this here...?"

He smiled. "Nobody will know. We're clothed, aren't we? And if I have to wait to touch you, I'll explode."

"We can't have that." She ran her fingers through his hair, her nails lightly scoring his scalp.

He played with her, letting her grow even wetter against his fingers, and he could smell her arousal. His cock pushed against the zipper of his jeans. Tense with desire, he forced himself to move slowly, to draw this out. He wanted to watch her face when she came from his fingers inside of her. He pushed a single finger inside of her tight sheath, and he watched as she bit her lip, her eyes closed in ecstasy.

His thumb rubbed around her clit with butterfly-light touches. Not enough to take her over the edge, but only to intensify her desire. She mewled in the back of her throat. Hooking his finger so it angled against that perfect spot inside her, he felt her start to tremble all over. He rubbed her clit harder. Her eyes flew open, and they gazed at each other as she finally started coming, her body shaking and quivering, her sheath milking his finger with every spasm.

"There you go. You're so beautiful, so amazing. I could watch you do this all day and night." He kissed her as she started to come down.

As she started to come back to her senses, she kissed him harder. To his delight, she began to unbutton his pants and, after pulling down the zipper, stroked him through his boxers. He tipped his head back. The hot sun, the smell of sex, and the weight of Sara in his lap all coalesced to make him almost delirious. It didn't help when she licked at his lips as she stroked his cock.

If he weren't careful, he'd come in his boxers just like this. He moved her hand away, but only to pull himself free. Her eyes widened—probably out of some fear of being seen—but he just smiled.

"Move up on me—yes, like that." He groaned when she sat up and her sex just brushed his aching cock. Her sundress covered them both, although at this point, Harrison wouldn't care if everyone in Fair Haven saw them, he was that desperate for her.

With her hands on his shoulders, she sank down on him, inch by inch, until she was seated on him fully. She was so tight and wet that he didn't know how much longer he would last. It didn't help that she began to bounce on his lap, her breasts jiggling. He watched her, his desire only ratcheting up higher and higher.

"You feel so good," she moaned. "So full and hard inside me."

Sara picked her up pace, but Harrison wasn't going to let her do this alone. He thrust with her as she came down on his cock, and they set a desperate rhythm. The seat they sat on squeaked with every movement. They swore and gasped and begged, and Harrison felt his body tighten in preparation for his climax. It built and built until he was mindless with it.

He watched as Sara bit her lip right as her body started to shake. Her sheath contracted around his cock. "Are you coming, baby?" he murmured as he licked her throat.

She let out a scream, and he wrapped his arms around her to hold her steady. In only a few more strokes, he was coming too, and he filled her with pulse after pulse. He emptied himself inside of her until there was nothing left in him. She'd claimed all of him. He was hers completely and irrevocably.

They were sweaty and sated after that. Neither of them wanted to move from where they sat. They kissed sweetly, their lips moving softly against the other's, and something bloomed between them that set Harrison's soul ablaze. *I can never let her go*, he thought as he tangled his hands in her long, dark hair.

His heart wondered if this were love, and his brain wanted to answer that question. But he didn't want to label this feeling right now. He wasn't sure why—out of fear? out of ignorance?—but he did know that he couldn't let Sara out of his life.

They cleaned up and settled back on the seat again. Harrison would need to take them back to the harbor before the sun set, but he didn't feel any compulsion to end this day anytime soon. If he were honest with himself, he'd admit that this was one of the best afternoons he'd ever experienced, thanks to the woman in his arms.

"I love you," he said.

Her mouth parted in surprise, but she didn't say the words back.

His heart clenched, but he knew he'd wait for her. He knew the words were inside of her, wanting to be set free.

He then said, "Can I ask you something?"

She tilted her head toward him. "You suddenly sound very serious."

"I want to make us official, Sara. I know we've had our differences, but I care about you. A lot. I can't get you out of my head, even if I wanted to." He stroked her arm. "Be my girlfriend?" he asked with a grin. "As adolescent as that proposal sounds."

She smiled, too, but it was a surprisingly sad smile. She touched the corners of his mouth. "Are you sure?"

"Would I ask if I weren't?"

She didn't have an answer to that. Turning away, she gazed off into the distance, and Harrison felt as if she'd put up a wall between them already. Was it fear that made her so reticent? Or another reason entirely?

"Don't run away from me," he murmured. "Don't push me away because you're scared."

She flinched. "You don't know what you're talking about."

"I know exactly what I'm talking about. You always have excuses, always have reasons why we won't work. But what about all of the reasons that we do work? Do you think this kind of connection is common? Believe me, it's not."

"You don't have to tell me that. I was married to a man for years who did nothing but make my life difficult." After a moment, she sighed and settled back into his arms. "If I'm afraid, it's for legitimate reasons."

"I know, Sara. But we can't let our lives be ruled by fear."

She was quiet, and he just touched her with gentle fingers: her hair, her cheek, her arms. Giving into temptation, he kissed her, and he rejoiced when she kissed him back. She could try to act like she wasn't affected by him, but they both knew it was a lie.

"Be my girlfriend," he repeated. "And come to dinner with my family so I can introduce you."

Her entire face paled at that. "I don't think that's a good idea."

"Don't let my mom scare you. She's mostly all bark and no bite." Thinking about the blind date she set him up on, he added, "Well, sort of. But I can make her promise to behave. I want to show you off to my family."

Sara just shook her head, smiling. "If I say yes, will you stop badgering me?"

"Say yes to which parts?"

"All of it." Her smile widened at the look in his eyes. "Because I do want to say yes, you know."

"Then say it. Say yes. Make it official. Let's make it real."

Her eyes shone as she gazed down at him. Finally, in a quiet voice, she said, "Then, yes. I want it to be real with you."

∽

AS THEY WALKED BACK to Harrison's car, the sun setting behind
them, Harrison couldn't stop looking at Sara. The way she walked,
her hips swaying slightly with each step; the way she tilted her
face toward the sun, like a sunflower; the way her dress billowed
and then clung to her toned legs; the way her freckles became
darker when she'd sat in the sun for hours in the afternoon; the
way her lips remained red after so much kissing.

He couldn't stop himself from kissing her when they reached
the car. She looked so beautiful, the sun creating a halo around
her, that she was a temptation no man in his right mind could say
no to. She smelled like salt and woman, her lips soft. He didn't
know if he could come up with a metaphor that would truly
encapsulate his feelings for this woman. A drug, an elixir, manna
from heaven—or maybe she was more like water or air—something you needed to live, to flourish. She was his necessity.

"I'll take you home." He opened the car door for her, although
she didn't move to get in just yet.

"I had a good time today." At his eyebrow raise, she added, "A
great time. An amazing time? Now you're just wanting your ego
stroked."

"I'm always good with getting something stroked, baby."

She blushed scarlet, which just made him laugh. He drove her
home, and she took his hand and squeezed it as he drove. He
looked over at her, and the smile she gave him only made him fall
even harder for her.

14

"*Y*ou look beautiful." Harrison kissed Sara on the cheek before placing his hand on the small of her back. He guided her toward the front door of his parents' home, which in Sara's estimation, looked rather like the front door to a castle.

His parents' place was huge. She'd heard that the Thorntons' house was palatial, but when they'd driven up the endless driveway to the house perched on a hill overlooking the lake, her breath had left her body. The house was an older Victorian with a wrap-around porch and painted a dark blue, sensible yet pretty at the same time. Sara had no idea how many rooms this place had —ten? or more? The front yard consisted of steps trailing up to the front door, while the yard itself brimmed with flowers and shrubbery, including hydrangeas that seemed to be bursting with white and blue blossoms.

Her heart pounded so hard that she had to stop herself from clutching at Harrison's arm to keep herself steady. Her nerves had dissipated somewhat after she'd agreed to go to a family dinner, but now? Now she was reminded of the disparity between the two of them once again. He'd grown up in this house, had had birthday parties and Christmas and brought friends over here, never knowing what it was like to worry about his next meal or if his mom had remembered to pay the rent or if she'd spent any money he had saved on booze.

"This place is gorgeous," she said as they approached the front door.

He smiled. "It's a bit much, but I'll let my mom know you said so. She's the one who's kept it up all of these years, even after we all moved out and left the house."

Harrison opened the front door into what Sara could only term an actual entrance hall. A glittering chandelier hung overhead, and a table with a vase of tulips sat on the bright marble floor.

Sara heard footsteps, and then she saw a woman who could only be one of Harrison's sisters. They looked so alike that it made her chest ache.

"You're here! Oh, you must be Sara. It's so nice to meet you. I'm Jubilee." Jubilee held out her hand, and Sara took it with a smile.

"It's so nice to meet you. Megan told me that she just hired you to work for her at the bakery. She's my sister, you know."

"She's told me so much about you that I feel like we already know each other."

Jubilee took Sara's hand and led her further into the house, like they were the best of friends. She saw Harrison smile and shrug behind her as he followed.

She could barely pay attention to what Jubilee was saying as she took in the rest of the house, including a living room with expensive oak furniture and paintings on every wall. A fire crackled merrily in the fireplace as they passed by. Sara couldn't help but wonder how anyone really lived in a place like this. Where were the signs that people lived here? The scuffed floors, the broken locks, the bathtub that only had two temperatures of hot and extremely hot? This house seemed more like a museum, and she could only imagine the entire family perched on the furniture, never eating or drinking anything that might stain the upholstery.

"I'm not much of a baker," Jubilee was saying, "but Megan is nice enough to put up with me. I've gotten the cash register down now, so that's good."

"I'm sure you'll do great. Megan loves people who are assertive and don't need a ton of direction," Sara replied absently as her attention was snagged by a painting of an eighteenth-century aristocrat. He had on a white wig and, if she didn't know better, had a very tiny dog in his lap.

"It's my first job ever, which is kind of pathetic. I told Megan that, but she just said that she didn't care so much about experience but about reliability." Jubilee shrugged.

Sara was about to assure Jubilee that she had nothing to worry about when they entered the dining room. The table was set like something out of a fairytale, with gleaming china and bouquets and glass wear. A chandelier also hung overhead, and it gave the room a warm and glowing aspect.

At the table sat Caleb, who stood when Sara entered.

"Sara, you know my brother Caleb," Harrison said as she and Caleb shook hands.

"So nice to see you again," Caleb said. Sara couldn't help but trace his features for any similarities to Harrison. The brothers had similar bone structures and had dark hair, but Harrison was stockier where Caleb was tall and rangy.

"Thank you for inviting me," she replied. "I've heard so much about the famous Thornton dinners that I couldn't resist accepting."

Caleb snorted. "If you mean acting like we're some rich family out of an Austen novel, sure. Just be sure not to slurp your soup and you'll be fine."

At that reminder, Sara felt her smile freeze. She'd never eaten in a house like this, with people like this. The fanciest dinner she'd ever had was at an Italian place in Seattle that threw breadsticks at patrons.

Harrison's hand was warm on her back, and he stroked her spine. "You'll do fine," he murmured in her ear.

She nodded. She wished she could believe him.

Just because you grew up in a trailer doesn't mean you're any less of a person, she told herself. Logically, she knew that was true. Wealth didn't make you better or more interesting. That didn't stop her from feeling intimidated, though. She wished, suddenly, that Megan were here with her. Megan's brashness would help her get through this without fearing that she'd screw up or humiliate herself.

"You're here. Wonderful." In floated a woman who could be none other than Lisa Thornton. She wore pearls at her throat and an expensive silk dress, and she definitely didn't look like a woman who'd birthed six children. She smiled as she kissed Harrison on the cheek, and then she turned toward Sara.

"Sara, it's so nice to meet you," she said in dulcet tones. "We've all heard so much about you. Although isn't it strange that we've all lived in Fair Haven for so long but never met?"

Sara took Lisa's hand, noting that the woman had her nails painted a muted pink. "It's nice to meet you, too. Thank you for inviting me."

"Oh, I didn't invite you, my dear. My son here did. We generally don't invite people who aren't family to family dinners. Easier that way, which I'm sure you can understand."

"Mom," Harrison growled.

Lisa gave a slight shrug while Sara bit the inside of her cheek to keep from saying something nasty in reply. Or maybe so she wouldn't burst into tears. At this point, it could be either of those two reactions.

"Jubilee, are you really wearing that outfit tonight?" Lisa

clucked her tongue, effectively ignoring Sara completely. "Boots with a skirt? Sweetheart, I thought we discussed this."

"You did. But that doesn't mean that I agreed," Jubilee replied.

"Mom, leave off it. Jubi looks fine. Besides, this is just a *family* dinner, right?" Caleb said.

"I talked to Mark yesterday. He says that he'll be attending our next dinner, although he assures me that the reason he hasn't been here is because he's too busy with his ranch." Lisa said the word *ranch* like a person would say *leprosy*, and Sara had a feeling there was a story there, too.

"Mark is younger than Caleb," Harrison explained, "and he owns a horse ranch south of here."

"And what about your other siblings?" Sara knew there were two others—the twins, if she remembered correctly.

"Seth is in the Marines and is currently overseas. Lizzie is traveling with her band. Mom, didn't Lizzie say she was in Chicago this week?"

Lisa pursed her lips. "Who knows, with that girl. She never comes home. That's all I need to know." After moving a fork slightly more to the left, Lisa left to find Dave and to check on dinner.

Right as dinner was about to be served some ten minutes later, Sara met Dave Thornton, who looked like an older version of Harrison. He had a kind smile and welcomed her without pretense, which she appreciated. He sat down at the head of the table, Lisa to his left, and Harrison to his right. Sara sat between Harrison and Caleb, while Jubilee sat across from them next to Lisa.

Sara dug her fingernails into her palm to stop herself from trembling. She hated that she was so intimidated by not only this house, but by Lisa. She had a distinct feeling that Lisa wanted her to feel intimidated, which didn't help her nerves at all.

The dinner began, and wine flowed along with the conversation as they ate each course. Sara mostly spoke with Harrison and Caleb. Caleb was wry and sarcastic, and he and Harrison kept her entertained through the dinner.

"Harrison told me that he took you out on his boat," Caleb said in a casual tone. "Did you two have a good time?"

Harrison glared at his brother while Sara choked on her sip of water. Harrison patted her back. "We had a great time, didn't we, Sara?"

She nodded. As she remembered how much of a good time they'd had...her body heated and, when she looked up to see Lisa staring at them, she blushed scarlet.

"Caleb here is a joker. Did you know that he wet the bed until he was seven?" Harrison said.

Now it was Caleb's turn to choke on a beverage.

"It's true," Harrison said in a serious voice as he looked at Sara. "We couldn't let him go to summer camp because he'd just wet the bed. It was a really big problem for him."

Caleb tried to step on Harrison's foot, but Sara sitting in between them kept him from accomplishing that goal.

"Harrison here wanted to be a lifeguard but he didn't learn how to swim until he was *twelve* because he was terrified of drowning—" Caleb was cut off when Harrison managed to kick him in the ankle.

"Boys, boys, what are you talking about?" Lisa cried. "Really, how can the two of you consider yourself mature adults?"

Sara rather wanted to ask that same question, although she couldn't stop laughing, either. Catching Harrison's eye, she realized that he'd started the fight with Caleb to distract her. Her heart warmed as he winked at her.

Although Sara calmed enough to enjoy the dinner somewhat, she should've known that it wouldn't last. As they began the main course, Lisa fixed her eye on her.

"Harrison tells us you're a teacher now," she said. "What grade do you teach?"

"Third grade. They're young enough to still like their teacher but old enough that I don't have to worry about anyone wetting their pants."

Everyone but Lisa laughed.

"And you have a son? From your previous marriage?"

Sara wasn't sure where this Q&A was going, but she refused to let Lisa see her sweat. At her side, Harrison was stiff, and she knew he wouldn't let his mom push Sara too far.

"Yes, his name is James, and he's six years old. He's the love of my life." She couldn't stop herself from looking up at Harrison after that, wanting to convey to him that he was as important to her now as her son.

He touched her hand underneath the table with a gentle caress.

"How nice. I remember hearing that you'd gotten married and had moved away. To Seattle, right? A shame that your marriage didn't last, though."

Sara froze while Harrison groaned, "*Mom.*"

"I'm sure he's a bright boy," Dave offered. "If his mother is any indication."

"How did you two meet?" Jubilee asked as she looked at Sara and Harrison.

Harrison raised an eyebrow, and Sara knew she'd have to reveal their connection, given that he couldn't announce he'd treated James. "James suffered from cancer when he was young. He's healthy now, but I wanted to make sure when something came up. That's how I met your brother."

Jubilee's expression seemed to close, and Sara remembered that she'd suffered from cancer as a child, too. "I'm sorry you had to go through that. What kind of cancer, if you don't mind me asking?"

"Neuroblastoma."

Jubilee's face became sad. "Did you know I had leukemia?"

"Really, Jubilee, this isn't the time or the place to talk about such things," Lisa said.

Sara saw that Caleb looked like he was about to say something cutting, but he controlled himself. Suddenly the table had turned painfully uncomfortable. Had Jubilee's cancer caused some kind of rift in the family?

"I'm glad to see you healthy now," Sara offered with a kind smile. "I know as a mother, that having your child diagnosed is a terrible thing, but I still didn't have to suffer through the chemotherapy or radiation."

Jubilee shrugged, but Sara could see that it wasn't a topic the young woman wanted to discuss over dinner. Considering Lisa's look of frustration, Sara couldn't blame the girl.

"I had no idea that you met at Harrison's office. What an interesting coincidence." Lisa drank a sip of her wine, gazing at Sara over the rim. "You don't run into eligible bachelors of his caliber every day, and especially not ones like him. You must've thought yourself very lucky to gain his attention at all."

"If anyone was lucky, it was me," Harrison said. "Sara is an amazing woman, and I admire her greatly."

"Of course you do, Son. But that doesn't negate the fact that you are also a very *eligible* man in a variety of ways. I'm sure Sara realized that and used that to her advantage, if you understand my meaning. And considering where and how Sara grew up, it makes sense." Lisa gave Sara a cutting smile, which went straight to Sara's heart.

Silence fell around the table. No one knew what to say. Sara felt Harrison vibrating with anger next to her, while she only stared at her plate and wished she could be sucked into the ground for all eternity. Humiliation washed through her, so painful that she could barely catch her breath.

Oh God, she thinks I'm only dating him for his money and connections. Because I'll only ever be white trash Sara Flannigan to her.

"You're being extremely rude, Mom," Harrison finally said. His body was tight next to Sara, and she felt his fist clench underneath the table. "You have no right to insult Sara like that. She's *my* guest. Since when did we treat guests like this?"

"Son..." Dave said while placing a warning hand on Lisa's arm. "Let's discuss this after dinner."

Sara looked up to see Jubilee with her mouth parted in shock. When their gazes met, Jubilee mouthed *I'm so sorry*, her cheeks red with embarrassment. Next to Sara, Caleb was shaking with anger just like Harrison.

"Why do you always do this, Mom? Can't we have a normal dinner for once?" Caleb tossed his napkin onto the table in disgust. "Sara, I'm sorry about all of this. You haven't done anything wrong. Our mother—well, I'll keep the term to myself, if you don't mind."

At that, Dave erupted, calling for Caleb to apologize to his mother. Lisa sniffled and wiped her eyes with her napkin. Harrison just shook his head. Sara wondered if she could run out without anyone noticing her doing so.

Harrison took her hand. "Come on. Let's get out of here. I'm not going to have you sit here and be insulted."

But for some reason, Sara couldn't stop herself from wrenching her hand from his grip. She didn't want to be led away like some pathetic child who couldn't defend herself. She didn't want his pity, or Caleb's or Jubilee's, and she most definitely didn't want Lisa to feel like she'd won some kind of battle here. Standing up, Sara looked straight at Lisa. The table fell into silence once more.

"You don't have to remind me of my past or my family. It follows me wherever I go," Sara said quietly, her chin tipped up in defiance. "But I'm not ashamed of my past. What *is* shameful is how you treat people you deem beneath you. I may be from the wrong side of the tracks, but at least my conscience is clear."

She didn't wait for any reply. Almost running from the room, she burst through the front door into the cool night air, gasping for air. She couldn't breathe. Anxiety pressed down on her until she almost choked with it. *I can't believe I just did that*, was all she thought as her mind spiraled. Sara hated confrontation of any kind, but her anger had gotten the better of her.

She didn't feel guilty, though. She felt relieved. Empowered.

Yet the initial high of telling Lisa Thornton to go to hell faded quickly. Here she was, standing in the family's sprawling garden, and behind her was the house that symbolized every reason why she and Harrison couldn't be together.

The gulf between them was too wide. How could they manage to cross it with obstacles like these? She pulled out her phone, tears blurring her vision, as she called a cab to come get her.

"Sara!" Harrison called out as he followed her into the garden. "Jesus Christ, I'm so sorry about all of that. If I'd had any idea my mom would say shit like that—"

Sara stopped him. "It's not your fault. I think everyone was as surprised as you."

"I can't believe she would do that. She's a piece of work, but that..." He shook his head, and he looked simultaneously shocked and enraged. And embarrassed. "God, I'm so sorry." He then tried to embrace Sara, but she resisted. He frowned down at her.

"I can't—I can't do this," she said in a wrenching voice. "I can't keep swimming upstream with no break in sight."

He stilled. "What are you saying?"

"I'm saying that I can't do *this,*" she said, waving her hand at them both. "I can't be with you."

"Why? Because my mom is a lunatic? I'm sorry that happened. I'm so angry I can't even look at her, but don't let her stop us. You can't let her come between us."

"But don't you see? She already is in between us. She'll come between us no matter what we do. She's never going to accept me, and I'm tired of fighting, Harrison. I fought to keep my marriage alive, I fought to keep my son alive, and now I'm going to have to fight to keep our relationship alive?" She shook her head. "What happens on the day you end up resenting me for separating you from your family? When you decide that you agree with your mom?"

He just shook his head before running his fingers through his hair. "I can't believe what you're saying. That I'd *agree* with anything my mom says."

"Maybe you don't now. But when you realize how much you've lost because of me, you will."

They stared at each other. Sara bit back the tears that threatened, and Harrison's expression was etched in stone.

"Don't do this, Sara," he pleaded. "This isn't the right way."

She just shook her head. The cab began pulling into the driveway, and when Harrison saw it, he grabbed her wrists.

"Don't leave. Not right now. We need to talk about this."

She wanted to pull away, but she didn't have the energy. Her heart splintered into pieces as she replied, "I have to. Don't you understand? I can't keep doing this."

His gaze roved over her face, searching, desperate. Finally: "Don't leave without me, then. I'm not going to let you be alone."

The fight went out of her right then; she let him embrace her. After Harrison paid the cab and sent him on his way, he ushered her to his own car.

As they were about to leave, though, Caleb came out of the house and knocked on the driver's side window. Harrison rolled it down as Caleb stuffed his hands in his pockets.

"Mom's pretty upset," he said. "Although not sure why, considering she instigated the whole thing." He peered into the dim light at Sara's face. "You doing okay?"

She shrugged. "I'll be okay. Sorry I ruined everyone's dinner."

"You didn't ruin anything," Harrison said. Looking at Caleb, he added, "I'll talk to you later. You'll take care of Mom? Because I can't talk to her right now."

Caleb nodded, stepping away so Harrison could reverse the car before driving off into the night.

15

*H*arrison didn't try to break the silence as he drove Sara back to his place. He should've known that taking her to a family dinner would be disastrous. Lisa had never supported his dating Sara, but he never could've imagined his mom would say something as terrible as that. He winced, anger bubbling up inside him again on Sara's behalf.

He didn't know if he'd ever be able to forgive Lisa for her behavior tonight.

Harrison's home was situated about twenty minutes away from his parents', a modern bungalow with floor to ceiling windows and a contemporary look that was the complete opposite of his parents' aesthetic. He preferred clean lines and muted colors, and when he'd bought this house, he'd loved it because it didn't look like something his mother would want to live in.

Is my entire life just rebelling against my parents? he thought darkly. He helped Sara out of the car. She looked up at him with a defeated expression, which only made him angrier toward his mother.

Once they were inside, he had her sit down in the living room. Taking her hands, he rubbed her fingers. "You want anything?"

She shook her head. "I'm okay. I feel like I overreacted back there, and now I'm kind of embarrassed." She rubbed the back of her neck.

"If you overreacted, then I definitely did the same. Come on, I need a beer, and I bet you could use something to drink, too."

He poured her a glass of white wine while he opened a bottle of beer. They toasted, and the quiet of his house combined with the alcohol allowed them both to relax. Sara snuggled against him, and he kissed the top of her head.

They stood with their arms around each other with no need to speak. What was there to say? Harrison wanted to apologize a thousand times over, but it wouldn't erase Lisa's words. Did she really hate the Flannigans so much that she'd humiliate a guest in her own home? He could barely comprehend it. His mother had never been the most welcoming of people, but she'd never stooped this low. He wondered, again, of how little he really knew his parents at the end of the day.

"Have I said how sorry I am? Because I am," he said.

"Don't apologize for something that wasn't your fault." Tilting her head back, she murmured, "Make me forget, Harrison."

He stroked her jaw. "I didn't come here to seduce you, you know."

"Maybe not, but I definitely came here to seduce *you*."

She stood on her tiptoes and kissed him, tasting of wine. He trailed a hand down her spine until it settled right above her ass. They kissed, lengthy and slow kisses, like they had all the time in the world with each other.

Harrison refused to think about her words from earlier. *I can't do this anymore.* He didn't want to consider that this could be their last night together. He pressed her closer, setting his beer down on the counter where her wineglass sat. When he licked inside her mouth, she made that noise that he loved so much. God, he loved her. He'd never expected to feel like this about someone so soon, but he knew Sara Flannigan had captured his heart since he'd first seen her in his office weeks ago.

"I love you," he murmured before kissing her throat.

She moaned. And then to his utter delight, she replied, "I love you, too."

He looked down at her.

She smiled tremulously. "I'm sorry I didn't say it before. I don't know why I didn't say it. I think I was just scared."

"I know. I'm just glad I know now." He kissed her forehead, her cheeks, her nose. And then he kissed her lips, and then he kneeled down to lift her into his arms. Carrying her to his bedroom, the moment seemed holy almost, like they were a part of something much larger than themselves.

He wanted her to forget everything that had happened this evening. He wanted her to forget that Lisa thought she wasn't good enough, or that she didn't deserve him. If anyone didn't deserve someone, he didn't deserve *her*. She was goodness and light and sweetness and he couldn't get enough of her no matter how hard he tried.

He wanted to apologize for the thousandth time, but she just put a finger to his lips and shook her head.

They stripped out of their clothes, wanting to be as close as possible. After stripping her of her bra and panties, he drank in her naked body. Her breasts, her softly rounded belly. Her creamy thighs, even her ankles that led to dainty feet.

He kissed her neck before biting it, leaving a mark. She did the same to him, and it only stoked his desire higher.

"I want to be inside you. I want to be inside your heart, where you can never get me out. That I'm so much a part of you that you can't breathe or eat without me." He didn't even know what he was saying, but the words came tumbling out like a waterfall.

She ran her fingers through his hair. "You're already there," she whispered.

After that, there was no more reason to say a word.

SARA SAW a desperation in Harrison's eyes that she hadn't seen before. She didn't know if it was due to what had happened tonight, but he dragged his fingers down her body, touching every inch of her skin. He kissed the inside of her elbow; her wrist; the indentation of her lower belly; the soft patch of skin between her thighs. She fell into a haze of desire, her body completely taken over by this man.

She didn't want to think anymore. She wanted to forget everything that had happened and somehow fall into the fantasy that they could shut out reality here in this bedroom. Maybe if she closed her eyes, she could make it happen. But when she did, she saw Lisa Thornton's face as she uttered those words across the dinner table.

I'm sure Sara realized that and used that to her advantage, if you understand my meaning. And considering where and how Sara grew up, it makes sense.

Fear bloomed inside her chest. Had she been unconsciously attracted to Harrison because of his wealth and the promise of financial security? Her thoughts were so jumbled that she wasn't even sure of the answer anymore. Lisa had gotten under her skin and burrowed there, and every chance she got, she drew blood. Sara tried to push the anxiety away, but Harrison still noticed that something was wrong.

He touched her face. "What is it?"

"I don't know," she replied in a plaintive voice. "I'm so mixed up right now."

"About what? What's there to be unsure of?"

She didn't want to admit that she was afraid Lisa was right. She shrugged, but she let her gaze wander to the ceiling as she did it.

"Sometimes I feel like nothing I do is right. Like every move I make, there's something or someone there to tell me I'm screwing things up."

"Is being in bed with me somehow wrong?"

She gazed into his dark green eyes, seeing the hurt there. The anxiety. The anger. "No," she said quietly. "I would never think this was anything but beautiful. But that doesn't stop the world from judging us anyway."

"Fuck the world," he growled. "They aren't in this bedroom. *We* are. And I don't give a damn about their opinions."

He kissed her, hard and hot and hungry, and she could only surrender to the tidal wave. He cupped her breasts, brushing her nipples with his thumbs as his tongue slicked inside her mouth. He was relentless in his assault, taking over each of her senses with a ruthlessness that set her body aflame. Moving downward, he took a nipple into his mouth and then laved it before blowing cold air on it. Sara moaned. He was so good at making her want him, want *this*.

But she needed more, and she wanted to taste him, too. She moved so they were face to face again, and then she kissed his chest, feeling the prickle of chest hair underneath her fingertips. He shuddered when she dragged her nails down his abdomen. His cock was hard and jutting, and she wrapped her fingers around him in sheer delight. This manifestation of his desire for her never failed to make her heart pound faster. She stroked him, feeling him grow larger against her palm.

"Keep that up and this will be over before you know it," he growled in her ear.

She just squeezed him harder.

He muttered her name before he pushed her curious hands away. She pouted, but she didn't have long to be upset. Pushing her onto her side so he lay along her back, spooning her, he lifted her leg so it rested on his hip and opened her completely to his touch. She blushed furiously as his fingers touched her soaked core, although she could only push back against him, begging for more.

"I need you inside me. Please, Harrison." She bucked and squirmed, dislodging his fingers.

He laughed darkly, but then she felt the tip of his cock press against her entrance. They both groaned at the sensation, and Sara let out a desperate sound when he filled her completely. She felt stuffed, overwhelmed, and her heart fluttered like a trapped bird within her chest.

Harrison didn't move for a long moment. Instead, he delved between her folds to find her swollen clit, and he began to tap it in light strokes. But he didn't move, and the touch of his finger only drove her higher and higher.

"Oh my God, what are you doing?" She gripped his hip, but he only shook his head.

"I want to feel you come around me first." He rubbed her clit harder, and she was so far gone that she couldn't be embarrassed by the sounds she made. Mewling, pathetic sounds, sounds that she'd blush over later on when she remembered. But right now, she only could feel her body tightening around his cock as he rubbed and rubbed, and then her orgasm slammed into her. She screamed, her body bowing backward, but Harrison just held her close. He licked at the back of her neck as he kept lightly touching her, and Sara shuddered seemingly endlessly.

When she let out the breath she hadn't even realized she'd been holding, Harrison pulled out, only to thrust hard inside her. So soon after her orgasm, she was beyond sensitive, and the feeling of him filling her again and again was almost too much. Her nerves flared and her pulse went into overdrive, and she kept hearing someone speaking when she realized she was the one talking.

"Please, please, please don't stop, don't stop, oh my God," she said in a litany.

Harrison just pulled her leg higher up on his hip, thrusting inside her. His chest was slicked with sweat, and the room smelled of sex and salt. Entwining their fingers together, Sara knew she was close to coming a second time. With each stroke of his cock, she spiraled higher.

She felt him reach his peak first. His cock twitched inside of her, and it was enough to set her off a second time. His teeth scored her neck; she moaned and writhed, her shudders shaking the bed. He filled her in never-ending spurts, and she couldn't help but foolishly wish that he'd marked her for eternity in this way, filling her with a seed that would eventually bear fruit.

They collapsed onto the bed, sweaty and replete. Sara rolled over so they faced each other. She touched his face, his lips, and she loved the way his beard scratched against her fingertips. She traced his eyebrows, dark like raven's wings. He kissed her fingers, which only made her heart squeeze with emotion.

"I love you," he said.

She smiled. Tears threatened for some reason, but she swallowed them back. "I love you," she replied.

As he leaned down to kiss her, she had this feeling in her stomach that this wouldn't last. That this would be the final time they held each other like this, kissing and touching and loving. That soon he wouldn't gaze down at her with that look in his eyes, but instead see her with the same disdain everyone else saw her with.

Harrison fell into a deep sleep soon after, but Sara lay awake beside him until the wee hours of the morning. Restless and edgy, she wanted to leave this house and run far away. How did she already feel trapped by everything that happened?

No, not trapped. Terrified. She looked at Harrison as he slept, his face lax and peaceful, and she wished with all of her heart that they could be together. As her eyelids finally became heavy and she fell into a fitful sleep, she vowed to herself that she wouldn't let anyone come between them, even as she feared that no matter how hard she tried, that it wouldn't matter in the end.

HARRISON DROVE Sara home in the morning, and he couldn't help but notice how quiet she was on the way there. He thought they'd worked out what had happened last night, but now he couldn't stop the doubts from flooding him.

Does she want to end things? Does she think that I'll really end up thinking about her like my Mom thinks I will?

He pushed the thought far away, disgusted. His mom was so far off it was absurd, but he also knew that Sara had a tendency to run when things got complicated. She protected herself—and her son, by extension—when she did this, but it also kept her from diving into the deep end in life. She'd keep herself walled away from all of humanity if she thought it would keep her heart safe and intact.

He stopped the car in front of her house. Sara unbuckled her seatbelt and opened the door without a word.

"Hey," he said, touching her hand. "Tell me what's wrong."

A shrug. "Nothing." At his look, she squeezed his fingers. "I'm okay. I'm just thinking about all I need to get done today."

"You're not regretting last night, are you? Because you shouldn't. No matter what my mom says."

He saw a flash of fear in her eyes, and it made his chest tighten.

"I don't regret anything," she said, but she wouldn't look at him when she said it.

"Good, because you shouldn't. We're going to be together no matter what people might say. I love my mother, but she does not rule my life." He quirked a smile. "You're lucky, though. A lot of sons would be too scared of my mother to tell her no."

Sara smiled back, but it was a tight smile. "Makes sense. Your mother is rather terrifying."

"She means well. Well, sort of. It's complicated." He ran his fingers through his hair. "Anyway, I'll talk to you later, okay? Don't let what she said get to you. She was projecting her own issues onto us."

Sara nodded, but her goodbye was a quiet murmur as she got out of the car. Her shoulders slumped as she walked toward her front door. Harrison suddenly wanted to catch her up in his arms, put her back into his car, and drive. Drive far, far away, so far that they forgot everything and everyone who had hurt them or made their lives difficult.

Except life didn't work like that. You could run, but you couldn't hide from your problems. He knew that, yet he had this niggling feeling Sara was stubborn enough to avoid things she found too scary to deal with.

"Sara, wait!" He followed after her.

She stilled, her key in her hand.

He didn't even know what he wanted to say. Grinning, he said, "I love you. In case you didn't hear it the first time."

But for whatever reason, that declaration didn't put a smile on her face. Instead, he swore he saw the shimmer of tears in her eyes. She leaned up to kiss him and, without a word, went inside her house.

He didn't know how long he stood there, staring at her front door, hoping against hope it wasn't the newest metaphor for their relationship.

16

*S*ara had experienced a number of surprises in her life, but nothing quite surprised her as much as seeing Lisa Thornton waiting outside her school to speak with her.

When Sara stopped in her tracks, James tugged on her arm. "What are you looking at, Mom?"

It had been three weeks since the infamous dinner, and it had been three of the happiest weeks of Sara's life. She and Harrison spent as much time together as possible, and he had taken her and James on a picnic near the lake last weekend. James had chattered the entire time about school, his friends, and anything else that popped into his head, but Harrison hadn't seemed to mind. Sara couldn't help but fall further in love with him when he interacted with her son. When James asked Harrison to show him how to fish one day, Harrison had said yes immediately, even asking Sara later if she would mind him taking James out for a guys' day eventually.

Kyle had never shown any kind of interest in his son, so seeing Harrison with James, a boy not even his own flesh and blood? She knew she'd found a keeper.

Now, though, she stared in wonder at the appearance of the woman who she simultaneously feared and hated. Harrison had refused to talk to his mother since the incident in solidarity with Sara, which she had appreciated immensely. Lisa had, apparently, been unwilling to apologize for what she'd said.

"Sara," Lisa said as she approached. She wore a cream suit with maroon pumps, her hair in a neat bun. She looked pale, and if Sara cared about this woman, she'd pity her for the obvious sadness hanging about shoulders. "Can we talk?" Lisa asked in a quiet voice.

Sara considered. She didn't owe Lisa anything, but at the same time, if Harrison's mom wanted to apologize, Sara would at least listen. The Thorntons were a tight-knit clan, and this kind of a split between the eldest son and matriarch had to be hurting everyone.

"I can't right now," Sara replied, because it was the truth. She gestured toward James. "I have to take my son home."

"Then can we speak at your house? Or perhaps meet for coffee once you get your son home?"

"Mom, who is this?" asked James.

Sara didn't particularly want Lisa to know her son, but out of politeness, she introduced the two. James's face lit up when he realized Lisa was Harrison's mom, but Lisa's stiff posture put everyone at a distance. Confused, he hung onto Sara's arm and fell silent.

"If you'd like, you can come to my home in an hour." Sara said the words like a dare. She knew Lisa would hate to be seen in Sara's neighborhood. She expected her to decline, despite asking to come over in the first place.

"That's fine. What's your address?"

Sara gave it, albeit reluctantly, and then shepherded James to her car. Once they were inside the vehicle, he started on his litany of questions that she knew had been about to burst out of him. "Is she really Harrison's mom? Why did she look so sad? Why does she want to come over?

Should I show her my bug collection? Mom, why aren't you saying anything?"

Sara glanced over at James and then patted his knee. "Sorry, sweetheart. I'm distracted. When we get home, you can go out and play with Travis since it's such a nice day while I'm talking with Harrison's mom."

An hour later, Sara waited for Lisa's arrival. When she'd told Ruth about the meeting, Ruth had snorted, saying that nothing good could come of it.

"What do you think she's going to do? Give you a casserole in apology?"

"I don't think Lisa Thornton knows how to make a casserole," Sara had replied in a wry voice.

Ruth decided to take a walk while Lisa was here, although she'd offered to stay if Sara would prefer that. Sara told her mom she'd rather see Lisa alone, mostly because if Lisa were going to say something humiliating, she'd rather not have witnesses.

Now Lisa sat in Sara's tiny living room, looking decidedly uncomfortable. Sara offered tea or coffee, but Lisa had declined.

Sara's irritation only grew. Why had Harrison's mother come all the way here just to stare at her carpet? And what had happened to that woman from the dinner, so condescending and cruel? She didn't know what to do with this Lisa. This Lisa she could almost feel sorry for. She didn't want to feel sorry for this woman.

"I'm sure you're wondering why I'm here," Lisa began. "I've been thinking a lot lately, and I wanted to explain why I said what I said. Most of all, I wanted to sincerely apologize." The words were stiff, clearly rehearsed, but Sara couldn't help but notice the thread of sincerity underneath them.

"Thank you." Sara rubbed her hands against her jeans. "I appreciate your apology."

"Harrison hasn't spoken to me since the dinner, which I

imagine you knew. He's very angry with me. So is Caleb, and even Jubilee." Lisa smiled grimly. "My Juju-bee hates confrontation, so you can imagine my surprise when she pulled me aside to tell me how embarrassed she was by what I said."

Sara's eyebrows rose to her hairline. Even Jubilee had remonstrated her mother? Now, that was surprising. She'd assumed that Jubilee would keep silent. *Good for you, Jubilee. Looks like Megan is rubbing off on you in the best way.*

"I was angry that everyone was angry with me, but I'm too old to keep fighting against my family. I love my children, Sara. I hope you know that."

Sara had never doubted that. "I know."

"So I hope you know that part of the reason why I said what I said—albeit in a rude, insulting way—was for a reason." Lisa took in a deep breath. "Did you know that I was in much the same position as you when I married Dave? I was from the Harrison family, and we weren't exactly the type of people the Thorntons mixed with. My father was a field worker, and my mother was a maid to another family in town. We never had much money, and oftentimes we went without.

"When I met Dave, I knew he was the one. He was so handsome and charming, and smart, too. He was the valedictorian of our high school class. I'd known him since elementary school and had loved him from afar, but it wasn't until we were teenagers that he noticed me." She smiled, her look far away. "He didn't care about what his family would say, or how the town would react. He was fearless, but he also had never experienced what it was like to accept that you couldn't always have what you wanted. Or even what you needed."

Sara swallowed, her skin prickling as Lisa spoke.

"His family threatened to cut him off if we married. Like Harrison, he was the oldest son, and his engagement to me almost broke his mother's heart. I think she hated me until the day she died." Lisa fell silent.

"What happened after that?" Sara asked.

"We married, of course, and we paid for it. No one would let us buy a house, and no one would hire Dave for the longest time. We were outcasts in our own hometown, and we almost left. But we were both stubborn. We wanted to prove that we could survive without anyone's good opinion."

"That's terrible."

"It was terrible, but you know what was the most terrible thing?"

Sara shook her head.

"The loneliness was terrible. We had each other, of course, but our families wouldn't speak to us. My parents tried to support us, but they felt pressured to be silent about it. We didn't have friends. We faced comments, whispers, and sometimes harassment for what we'd done. People were convinced that I'd trapped Dave by getting pregnant, although Harrison was born an entire year after we'd married." She smiled grimly. "It didn't matter what we said. We had to fight for years to regain people's respect, and some days Dave would look at me like he'd regretted what he'd done. When you're wondering if you should pay rent or buy food, but you can only choose one of those two things? When you can't give your wife the life you had promised her? I think he wished he'd given into his family's demands. He never said the words, but I could see it in his eyes all the same."

Sara didn't know what to say. Her heart pounded in her ears, and part of her didn't want Lisa to continue speaking.

Lisa looked her straight in the eye as she said, "I'm telling you this because I wanted to warn you. This road you've taken with my son? It won't be easy. You may think it's a new age, and no one will mind. Perhaps you're right, but you should know that Harrison is destined for great things. Things outside this tiny town, and seeing him held back from accomplishing those things would break my heart. Do you really want to be responsible for holding him back?"

Sara didn't know where her calm came from. Maybe she was so tired of fighting that she didn't have the energy anymore. "Are you saying that I'm only a millstone around his neck?"

"I'm saying that I know what it's like to try to overcome public opinion. You will always be Sara Flannigan, and he will always be Harrison Thornton. You are people from different worlds. Trying to change that may very well result in heartbreak." Lisa leaned forward, her expression tightening. "I also know that you were the subject of...rumors, when you were younger."

Sara felt her throat tighten. Humiliation washed through her, and she couldn't stop the memories from flooding back.

She's a slut who'll sleep with anything that moves.

How many of the football players did you screw, Flannigan?

Whore.

"And we both know where there's smoke, there's usually fire," Lisa continued. Her initial gentle tone vanished, and now she replaced it with the hardness that Sara had come to expect from the Thornton matriarch. "Don't make Harrison's life harder because you're being selfish. I would say the same thing to him, too. Sometimes you have to accept that not everything can go the way you want it to. And at the end of the day, do you want my son to blame you for all of the troubles you're going to endure?"

Sara wondered if you could die of embarrassment. But to her frustration, she remained very much alive as she stared at Lisa Thornton, sitting in her living room like some kind of pale soothsayer. Had the apology been a lie? Or was it somehow tangled together with her belief that the two of them truly were better apart?

Standing up, Sara said in a stiff voice, "I think I fully understand why you've come here. I must ask you to leave, though. I have things I need to take care of." It was a dismissal through and through, but she didn't care that she was being blatantly rude.

Lisa didn't seem fazed. "I appreciate your willingness to speak with me. Have a nice afternoon."

Sara didn't show Lisa out. Once the front door closed, she collapsed onto the couch, staring at the ceiling. Her head pounded, and she couldn't get her thoughts in order. Why had Lisa come here at all, except to tell Sara what she already knew?

"Hey, can I come in?" James came inside and then stopped in his tracks when he saw Sara. "Are you crying?"

Sara realized with a start that she was crying. Wiping the tears away, she tried to smile. "Let's get you some lunch, buddy. Does a bologna sandwich sound good?"

James just frowned at her in confusion. To Sara's heartbreak, he entwined his fingers with hers as they went into the kitchen.

"Don't worry, Mom. We'll be okay. I'm older now, so I can help."

His voice was so earnest that she almost dissolved into tears. She just hugged him close.

AFTER HARRISON CALLED and left a voicemail for Sara a fifth time in a row with no response, he decided it was time to see her for himself. Either she was avoiding him, or something was seriously wrong.

On a Thursday evening, he knocked on her front door, only to have Ruth Flannigan answer the door. The older woman didn't seem distraught, so Harrison knew that Sara had been avoiding him. He scowled. Ruth raised a brightly dyed eyebrow.

"Is Sara here?"

"She is, although she's putting James to bed right now."

"Tell her I'll wait out here to speak with her."

Ruth seemed like she wanted to protest, but at his dark look, she nodded. Pacing back and forth on their tiny porch, he forced himself to stay calm. There could be a very good reason why she hadn't called or texted him. Maybe her phone had died and she hadn't gotten a new one yet. Maybe her phone just wasn't charged.

Maybe after everything that had happened, she didn't want to see him again.

When Sara stepped outside, she looked sad. Tired.

"What are you doing here?" she asked in a quiet voice.

"Are you all right? You haven't responded to any of my calls." He tried to embrace her, but she put up her hands.

Not a good sign. His heart caught in his throat.

"I'm fine. I needed to think. So much has happened..." She looked away.

The moon was a tiny sliver in the sky, and Harrison focused on it to keep his bearings. "I was worried about you."

"I know. I'm sorry. I should've called. I just didn't have the energy, I guess."

"So talking to me only drains you?" He couldn't keep the hurt from his voice. "What the hell happened since the last time we saw each other?"

She opened her mouth, but shut it a second later. Had someone spoken to her? Or did she doubt their relationship— their love—so much already that she thought it should end?

His blood ran cold. "Sara," he said slowly. "What is this really about?"

"I've thought about this long and hard, and I think—I think we should end this."

There it was: the words he'd been dreading and yet, somehow expecting. Gazing down at her face, he felt rather like he'd been thrown into the eye of a hurricane. Tossed around, and yet standing still amidst it all.

"Are you going to give me a reason why we should break up?" he growled.

She shook her head. "I think the reason is clear. We aren't good for each other. We're too different. We come from separate worlds. Do you really want to fight every single day of our lives?"

"Hell yes, I do. I'll fight until my dying breath for you. The question is: why won't *you* do the same?" He saw tears shining in her eyes, and he drew away. Stuffed his hands into his pockets. "Don't answer that, actually. I don't want to know the answer."

"I love you, Harrison. I do. But I know when to put up the white flag, too. The thought of holding you back is too much to bear."

"The thought of holding me back?" he echoed. Suddenly, anger flared inside of him. He wanted to shake her, make her see sense. He gritted his teeth. "If that's what lets you sleep at night, Sara. But you know what I think is happening? I think you're scared. You're terrified of what this is, and you'd rather toss it away than fight for it. If you really loved me, you'd fight tooth and nail for our love, not set it aside because it's inconvenient."

Her face flushed, tears falling down her cheeks. "Don't you dare call me a coward, Harrison Thornton! You have no idea how long I've had to fight. I've had to fight just to live since I was a child. Do you know what it's like to worry about what you're going to eat because your mother spent all of your money on alcohol? When you worry that your little sister might get frostbite because all of your socks have fallen to pieces? When you lay awake at night, terrified that you're going to have to pick out your son's coffin if he dies of cancer?" Her voice rose with each sentence, until she almost yelled. "How *dare* you. You have no right to accuse me of fear. I'm trying to end things before more people get hurt. If that makes me a coward, then so be it."

"So that's it, then? You've decided it's over, and I'm just supposed to go along with it?" He pressed closer to her until they were only a breath apart. "You don't get to decide that alone, Sara. You don't get to tell me that our love isn't important enough." He cupped her face, forcing her gaze to meet his. "I love you," he said, anguished. "Isn't that enough? Isn't that the only reason we need?"

Her bottom lip trembled, and he watched as tears rolled down her face. "It can't be enough when everyone else says it isn't," she whispered.

Wiping her tears away with his thumbs, he touched his forehead with hers. "It can be, if you let it."

"I'm sorry. I'm sorry, Harrison." Her voice was choked with sobs. "I do love you. But I can't keep doing this. Please don't make this worse than it already is."

He wanted to rail at her. He wanted to shake her, he wanted to yell at her, he wanted to kiss her until she melted against him. In a flash of fury and frustration, he did kiss her, opening her mouth and demanding that she respond. She made a little noise in the back of her throat, but she kissed him back. He tasted the salt of her tears.

Then she wrenched away. Shaking her head, she ran inside, shutting the door in his face.

17

*H*arrison kneeled down in front of Delilah, one of his latest patients to go into remission from leukemia. "This is going to be the last time we see each other for a while," he said, smiling. "You take care of your mom and dad, okay?"

Delilah, with her red cheeks and lips, looked like a porcelain doll. Except her predilection of jumping in giant puddles and throwing mud at her siblings generally destroyed any comparison with a breakable doll. The chemotherapy had caused her blond curls to fall out, but Harrison could make out glints of peach fuzz on her head.

The girl nodded solemnly, then reached inside her pocket to pull out some leftover Easter candy. "Thank you. My mom said I should say that. I wanted you to have some candy, too."

He bit his lip to keep a straight face. "Thank you," he said in a serious voice.

The candy was melted, but Harrison couldn't help but feel that it was the best part of his week so far.

As Delilah and her parents left his office, though, the depression and anger came flooding back with a vengeance.

Sara. He missed Sara like he missed a limb. Or missed his

heart. He hadn't seen her in a week, and every passing day had been torture. He'd called her more than once, to see if she'd rethink her decision, but she'd ignored every message. By the third ignored message, Harrison had decided that he'd sacrificed his pride enough. He wasn't going to beg Sara to take him back.

So he told his pride. His heart, though, wanted him to go to her front door and throw himself at her feet.

He inhaled a deep breath. He'd barely slept all week, and food tasted like ash in his mouth. The evenings had been filled with drinking with Caleb and Heath, although his brother and friend had given him a wide berth. He'd been grumpier than a wounded bear, lashing out at anyone he could. Caleb had finally had enough and had told him he could sit at home by himself if he was just going to rip into him every time Caleb opened his mouth.

Heath had been less confrontational, but even he had hinted that maybe Harrison needed to take a break. Take a break from what? he'd countered. *Maybe figure out how to move forward,* Heath had suggested.

Easier said than done, when the love of his life had decided that she didn't want to be with him because she was too terrified to commit.

When Harrison left his office later that day, he had planned to go home and drink alone. He hadn't expected to see Megan Flannigan, of all people, with an impatient look on her face as she waited by his car in his office's parking lot.

Megan was a pretty woman, with her flaming red hair and eyes that were the exact same shade of blue as her older sister's. She was taller than Sara, and she had a stubborn tilt to her jaw that Harrison knew had plagued anyone who'd gotten close to Megan. At the moment, she leaned against his car like she owned it. When he stepped up to her with a quizzical expression, she shrugged.

"I needed to talk to you," she said without greeting. "Thought this was as good as any place."

Glancing at the clouds overhead that threatened rain at any moment, he unlocked his car and gestured for her to get into the front seat. She did so without hesitation.

He turned the car on so the heaters began to blast hot air, and Megan sighed in relief. He couldn't stop the quirk of a smile at that sound, which sounded like Sara so much that it hurt.

"Are you going to tell me why you were waiting for me, or am I going to have to guess?" he finally asked.

She laughed a little. "Sorry, I was freezing out there." She rubbed her hands. "I'm here for my sister, but she has no idea I'm here. If she did, she'd kill me."

At the mention of Sara, Harrison stilled. What was Megan up to? But looking at her expression, he only saw sadness and, he hoped, a real desire to help.

"Sara's been a wreck since you guys broke up," Megan said without preamble. She let out a breath. "Crying, barely eating, not sleeping. She said that she cried in the bathroom at her work yesterday. She's a mess, and I hate to see her like that."

He swallowed against a dry throat. "Then why...?" The question was unspoken, but it hung there, waiting to be answered.

Why end things to begin with?

"I told her you didn't know about what had happened, but she refused to listen. She's so stubborn sometimes, I swear." She looked at his confused face and explained, "Your mom spoke to Sara the day you guys broke up."

Harrison felt two things at once: shock; and absolute, all-consuming rage. Gripping the steering wheel, he bit out, "*My mother?* What the hell did she say this time?"

"She basically told Sara that she needed to break up with you because Sara would ruin your life. She also talked about the rumors Sara suffered from when she was in high school, saying that people would bring those up again. Considering they already have..." She gave him a dark look. "Suffice to say my sister decided to be a martyr and put things to bed, so to speak."

He groaned. He saw Sara's stricken expression the last time they spoke, and his heart splintered anew. *What did my mom tell her? And why isn't it legal to strangle your own mother when she pulls something like this?*

Finding his voice again, he practically growled, "I'm not surprised. Disgusted, horrified, angry—but not surprised. My mother is a piece of work, and she's been showing her true colors lately."

"I figured as much. Sara said that I shouldn't get involved because things were over and done with, but she's miserable without you." Megan brushed her hair from her pale forehead. "I'll never be a fan of your family for various reasons, but I could see how happy you made my sister. She hadn't been happy in a long time. Not with her shitty ex-husband, or having to take care of James... She deserves happiness. And love. If you can give her that, I want you to be together."

Harrison knew such a speech couldn't be easy for a woman like Megan, who kept her heart under lock and key. But he also knew the deeply abiding loyalty inspired by a sibling, and he couldn't stop the growing respect for Megan as a result.

"Do you know what else my mother said?" he forced himself to ask.

"I don't know the specifics. Sara wouldn't tell me, but I was able to get some things out of her. And then our mom got some other things, and we put two and two together." She turned toward him, her eyes searching. "Do you love her?"

He didn't flinch. "Yes. With all of my heart."

"Good." She nodded, like she'd gotten the confirmation she'd wanted. "Then you're going to fight like hell to get her back, right?"

He smiled grimly. "You have no idea."

WHEN HARRISON STORMED INTO HIS PARENTS' home an hour later, he found his mother in the sitting room, reading a book, like she hadn't just ruined his life and Sara's. At his entrance, she raised a delicate eyebrow.

"What the *hell* did you say to Sara?" he snarled. He didn't care that she was his mother: what she'd done was unconscionable. Unforgivable. He could barely look at her right now.

At his question, he saw the first vestiges of her mask cracking. Trembling slightly, she set her book aside and replied, "Are you going to growl at me like a rabid dog, or will you sit down like an actual human being?"

He sat down.

"If you mean that I went to speak to that woman, you're correct. I did."

For some reason, he'd expected she'd deny it. He struggled to keep his calm, but it was nipping at his heels, bursting to get free. "Why?"

"Why? Why do you think? Harrison, consider for one second with a part of your brain for once. She's a Flannigan, her mother is an alcoholic, and for all you know, she *enjoyed* the entire football team as a teenager. She's nothing more than trash. Why would you ruin your future for someone like that?"

To his surprise, tears pooled in Lisa's eyes, like the thought of him with Sara truly broke her heart. Then again, the tears could simply be another means of manipulating him. He shook his head.

"I can't believe you would go behind my back like that and say things like that to her. She's done nothing to deserve your hatred. She's an intelligent, beautiful, thoughtful woman who adores her son. Those rumors you mentioned? Rumors started by Devin Yates because she dared to turn him down. If I'd known she was being treated like that in school…" He stood up again and pushed fingers through his hair. "I can't believe you would act like this. I'm ashamed to call you my mother."

She flinched. Closing her eyes, she took a deep breath. "Then why are you here?" she asked quietly.

"To know the truth. To see if my own mother would act like this. To demand that you apologize to Sara, and to a lesser extent, to me."

"I already apologized to Sara for what I said at dinner that night."

"Oh well, then I guess everything's okay now?" He shot her an incredulous look. "You amaze me. You know what, though? I'd already stopped talking to you, but this? This is too much. Unless you do something to right this wrong, I don't want anything to do with you."

She seemed almost frail as she asked, "What does that mean?"

"It means you're as good as dead to me."

She gasped, and then her tears fell in earnest. Although Harrison hated himself for doing nothing to comfort her, he couldn't. His anger and hatred for her actions overwhelmed every other feeling.

"You can't do this," she sobbed. "Harrison, I love you. You know that, don't you?"

"I love you, too, but that doesn't mean I should suffer this kind of treatment. And most definitely, Sara shouldn't have been treated like this. I love *her*. Did you ever stop to think about that?"

Dave came downstairs at the commotion, and seeing his wife crumpled on the sofa, crying, while his eldest son stood over her, he demanded, "What happened?"

"Your son has decided to break my heart, that's what," Lisa said as she tried in vain to wipe away her tears.

"Harrison, explain yourself." Dave sat down next to Lisa and pulled her into his arms, rubbing her back. "You're standing there and making your own mother cry like this?"

"Considering she told the woman I love that she's not good enough for me, I'm not going to apologize." Harrison clenched his jaw, although the disappointment in his father's face almost broke him. "I told her that she's dead to me."

Dave's eyes widened. "What?"

"You heard me. Until this is rectified, consider me no longer your son."

He turned to leave and as he approached the front door, he felt a touch on his arm. "Son, don't do this. We can talk this through. You know your mother is impulsive, but she means well."

"She means well! That's what everyone says!" He wrenched his arm away. Dave was Harrison's height, and almost his spitting image, although his once dark hair was now threaded with gray. "She went too far this time, Dad. Do you think I wanted this? I want to be with Sara, not have my own mother against us like this."

Dave rubbed his temples. "Look, I'll get the full story from her, but don't cut her—your family—out of your life. Don't. I've had my family turn their back on me, and it's unbearable." His expression was stricken.

Harrison could only shake his head. "I'm sorry, Dad."

Dave just looked at him, with the saddest expression Harrison had ever seen in his eyes. "So am I. Sorrier than you'll ever know."

HARRISON BARELY REMEMBERED the drive back to his house. He could only see images—Sara's face, Megan's, his mother's—and when he dragged himself inside, he had no idea how he was going to fix this. He'd broken with Lisa, but would that be enough for

Sara? Beautiful, stubborn Sara? Who'd been hurt so much in life and was terrified to trust?

He knew now that Sara had broken up with him because she was afraid he'd turn on her like Lisa had said he would. Logically, he understood that. Emotionally, he wanted to kiss her, touch her, hold her, until she understood that he'd never leave her.

He got a beer out of his fridge and tipped it back, letting the cool liquid slide down his throat.

Dad just called me. You want to talk? Caleb texted him.

Not really. What did he tell you?

That you got into a massive fight with Mom over Sara. What did she say to Sara? It must've been really bad this time.

Harrison gave in and called Caleb, recounting what he knew. Caleb swore into the phone and, by the time Harrison had given him the full picture, he said, "You know I'll stand by you. Mom went way out of line this time."

Harrison heard a noise, and then Jubilee spoke. "I'm with you guys, too!"

"Since when is Juju-bee with you?" Harrison asked wryly.

"Since she burst through my door and demanded I put my phone on speaker when I said I was talking to you. Jubilee, don't you have your own apartment?"

"Yeah, but your house is bigger. Besides, I need to borrow your drill."

"Oh geez." To Harrison, he said, "We're both here for you. Let me know if you want us to do anything."

"Thank you. Really. Just...keep Dad from hounding me for a while, okay?"

"We'll try," Jubilee said. "And Harrison?"

"Yeah?"

"Don't let Sara go. Go tell her you love her and you won't leave until she says she'll have you back. I know she wants to say yes."

Caleb: "How in God's name do you know that?"

Jubilee sniffed. "Woman's intuition."

Caleb and Jubilee squabbled, which amused Harrison enough to keep him from falling into a deeper pit of depression for the moment. After he'd told them goodbye, he cracked open another can of beer and finally sat down to figure out how the hell he was going to get Sara Flannigan back.

18

"*M*om, did you hear me? I said that I scored a goal today in PE."

Sara looked up from the cutting board where she was chopping carrots. James sat at the kitchen table, his chin in his hands as he watched her. "I'm sorry, what did you say?"

"I said that I scored a goal today."

"That's great, honey. Playing basketball?"

He rolled his eyes. "You don't score goals in basketball. It was soccer."

"Don't sass your mother," Ruth said as she entered the small kitchen. Wearing a purple blouse with matching purple pants, she looked like a veritable rainbow with her red hair.

"Sorry. But, Mom, you've barely been listening to me since we got home today. Every day you look sad. Why do you look so sad? Is it because Harrison hasn't come by and given you flowers?"

Sara returned to her carrots, shaking her head. She hadn't spoken to Harrison since that fateful night when she'd told him things were over between them. He'd called a handful of times afterward, but she'd ignored them. Soon, the calls and texts had dried up.

She told herself it was for the best.

"Why don't you go wash your hands and then get your homework out while I finish up dinner?" she said.

James shrugged and left the kitchen. From the corner of her eye, she wondered if her boy had grown in the last month. He'd be taller than her before she knew it.

"He's right, you know. You are sad all the time." Ruth sat down in James's vacated chair. "What can I do? Do you want me to beat up this guy?"

Sara laughed, but it was strained. "If you beat up anyone, it should be me. I was the one to end things."

"Really? Why? What did he do?"

"Nothing. He didn't do anything wrong. It's me. I'm all wrong for him." She chopped the carrots with more force, and a few flew off the board onto the kitchen floor. Cursing, she bent down to pick up the orange pieces.

"Sara, honey, do you really believe that?" Ruth's voice was anguished, and when Sara looked into her mom's eyes, she saw unshed tears behind her glasses. "How can you be wrong for someone who you love and who clearly loves you?"

Sara looked away. Tossing the carrot pieces into the trash, she stared at the cutting board for a moment. What was she going to chop next? Onions. She was going to chop onions. Tossing the carrots in a bowl, she set to work on the onion, but it only made her eyes water. Or perhaps they were just unshed tears that had been waiting for an entrance.

"I know that you went through hell. That when I was drunk and blacked-out, that you had to pick up the pieces. You'll never know how sorry I am for that. I can never make up those years to you, but I hope I can tell you now that you deserve to be happy." Ruth touched her shoulder.

"But don't you see?" Sara whirled around. "It doesn't matter what I want. His family will never accept me, and what happens when he realizes that he made a horrible mistake? What if he feels like he's trapped, and leaves me in the end?" She shook her head. "I can't trap myself in a marriage like that again. I can't do it again."

"Sara Denise Flannigan, I never took you for a coward."

Sara's eyes widened.

"Harrison Thornton is nothing like your deadbeat ex-husband, and everyone and their dog knows it. You know why?" Ruth pointed a finger at Sara's chest. "Because he loves you, and he's a decent, honorable man. I'd give my left hand for a man to look at me like that man looked at you. Like he'd move heaven and earth just to get you a bouquet of roses. Don't let your past dictate your future, otherwise you'll stay trapped in your pain for the rest of your life." Ruth's lips thinned, and her voice was hoarse as she said, "I've done it. I drank because I couldn't deal with the pain. Don't make my mistakes, Sara. For the love of God, don't."

Sara stared at her mom, at a loss for words. Ruth had never been this honest with her in all of the years she'd known her. Impulsively, Sara threw her arms around her mom and hugged her tight. Ruth only hesitated a second before she hugged her back.

"I love you, honey," Ruth whispered. "I know I've screwed up so much. I don't deserve your forgiveness, but that doesn't mean I don't want to see you happy."

"I love you, too." Sara hugged her tighter, needing to hold onto her mom for the first time in almost thirty years.

As they finally parted, laughing a little through their tears, they heard a knock on the front door. Sara's heart leapt. *Harrison? Had he come to see her?*

"I'll get it!" James called out.

"Go," Ruth said, putting Sara's hair to rights. "I bet that's him."

She nodded eagerly and almost skipped to the front door, but then she heard James say, "Oh, Dad. What are you doing here?"

Sara froze as she took in her ex-husband standing in the doorway. Kyle Daniels was a handsome man, in a cold kind of way, and when he looked up at her, he smirked at her. *Smirked.* Her excitement quickly transformed into wariness.

"Can I come in, or are we just going to talk for all of your neighbors to hear?" Kyle asked in a bored tone.

Sara heard Ruth come up behind her. It was James who finally answered his father's question. "You can come in, but dinner's almost ready, so you'll have to leave soon."

Sara coughed a laugh. They all entered the living room, with Sara, Ruth, and James sitting on one couch while Kyle sat on the large chair diagonal from the trio.

"James, come sit with your old dad," he said, waving at James. "I haven't seen you in ages."

James hesitated, and at the darkening look on Kyle's face, only sat back further against Sara. Sara rubbed his neck soothingly.

"I see you've pitted the boy against me. Fine. I'm not here for a social call." Kyle pulled out an envelope and tossed it onto the coffee table.

Sara said, "James, how about you go to your room—"

"Let him stay. He can hear this, too," Kyle interrupted. "I'm suing for full custody. You've made it difficult for me to see James by moving here, and I've gotten wind of your activities." He smiled a mocking smile. "Your past always catches up with you, doesn't it, Sara?"

"James, go to your room." Sara gently pushed her son off the couch, and it didn't take much to send him straight to his room. He did look over his shoulder at his mom once before going down the hall to his room.

"What the ever-living hell are you talking about?" Ruth demanded. "You never gave two shits about that boy, and now suddenly you want to *raise* him?"

Kyle was about to speak, but Sara interrupted him this time. "My mom is right. You've never been a part of James's life. Why are you doing this? And don't try to act like you're doing it in his best interest."

"Why else do you think I'm doing this? Clearly you're unfit to raise him." At Sara's confused look, he explained, "You think I haven't heard about what you've been doing up here? Trying to snag a rich husband? Gossip travels quickly in this day and age, and when someone told me that my ex-wife was throwing herself at none other than Harrison Thornton? I knew you were returning to your old ways."

Sara was shaking with anger, and she barely restrained herself from getting off the couch and punching Kyle in the mouth. "You know as well as I do that any rumors about me are false. You're doing this to punish me."

Kyle shrugged. "Does it matter the reason? You have no means to fight this, Sara. Either give in gracefully, or I'll drag this to hell and back again."

"You'll take my son over my dead body, you selfish piece of shit!" Sara stood up, only keeping her voice down so James wouldn't overhear. "You're pissed that I dared to leave you. Well, you know what? I'd leave you again. I'd leave you a thousand times over, you lying, cheating scum. Get out of my house before I call the cops."

Kyle slowly stood up, his own expression tight with rage. "Do you really think you can win this?"

"I know I can. I know any court will look at your past and see how unfit of a father you would be. You can't hide all of the facts, no matter how hard you try."

"Keep telling yourself that, but know this: I will take our son and you will have nothing. Nothing, you hear me? I should've left you when you told me you were pregnant. Hell, who's to say he's even mine to begin with?"

Sara snapped. Slapping him across the face, her hand stung from how hard she hit him. She vaguely heard Ruth gasp behind her. Kyle gazed up at her, his eyes menacing, but he didn't move to strike her. He wiped the smear of blood from his lip in a slow motion.

"You're nothing," he whispered. "You're nothing but trash that should've stayed in her place. You'll be sorry for this."

"Get out," was all she could say in reply.

Ruth finally got up, taking Sara into her arms. Kyle stalked out of the house and slammed the front door behind him.

No one said a word. Sara tried to catch her breath, but she didn't have any tears left. The only feeling left? Anger. And sheer determination.

"He's getting my son over my dead body," she said as she turned toward Ruth. "He's only doing this because he wants revenge."

"And I'll be right behind you with the shotgun. Just tell me when and where, honey."

That caused a startled laugh from Sara, and the two women started laughing together. It was better than crying. James heard the commotion and came into the living room.

"Is Dad gone? Are you laughing? Why were you yelling?"

Sara yanked James into a tight hug, which he allowed for a grand total of two seconds before wiggling free.

"Grandma, Mom's lost it. You should do something," he said in a solemn voice.

That only caused more laughter.

During dinner, Sara fell quiet at the table, listening to her mom and son chatter together. Although she wanted to slap Kyle again, she almost wanted to thank him, in a way. His words about her being nothing and deserving nothing?

She knew they were wrong.

She deserved better, and if she were brave enough, she could have what her heart truly wanted.

I want Harrison, her heart whispered. *I want to be with him, damn anyone who thinks otherwise.*

Because if she listened to the Kyles and Lisas of the world? She would be miserable. She would be alone, and she would be living in the past, just like Ruth had said she would.

Courage rose up inside her, although it was tempered with the fear that Harrison wouldn't take her back. She could hardly blame him. She'd told him that it was over between them, and then she'd completely ignored him when he'd tried to repair their relationship. She'd acted like his feelings hadn't mattered at all.

"Sara, you haven't eaten a thing," Ruth said with concern. She pointed a spoon at her still full bowl of soup. "You can't starve yourself, you know."

"I'm not very hungry, I guess."

"I'll eat it!" James plucked the bowl and started slurping the soup before Sara could react.

"Well, at least we know food won't go to waste around here," Ruth said.

By seven, James was yawning, and Sara told him to get ready for bed. She heard him splashing water in the bathroom, which generally meant he'd be in bed in about ten minutes or so. He had a tendency to waste time while washing his hands and brushing his teeth.

Sara knocked on his door a quarter after seven. She slipped inside and sat down on his bed. His room was filled with bugs— plastic bugs, thankfully—of all sorts: grasshoppers, butterflies, beetles, ants, and a few arachnids thrown in for good measure. His sheets were dinosaurs, and although Sara had offered to get him new bug sheets, James had declined. He'd probably use these dinosaur sheets until he was leaving for college, she thought with a smile.

His expression was worried, and his gaze darted over her face as he looked up at her. "Mom," he whispered, "is Dad going to take me away?"

Her breath caught. She took his hands in hers and squeezed. "No, honey. Of course not."

"But I heard him say..." His lower lip quivered. "I don't want to go. Please don't make me."

"Oh honey, no. I won't let that happen. Your dad, he just says things sometimes because he's angry. I'm sorry you had to hear us arguing."

"I think you should call Harrison."

Her eyes widened. "Why do you say that?"

"Because he's bigger than Dad, and he could definitely kick him around if he tried to take me away."

She bit back a laugh, especially as James was completely serious. "You think I should?" she asked just as seriously. "Do you miss Harrison?"

"I think you miss him. You've been sad, but when you talked to him, you were happy. So I don't get why you aren't talking to him anymore."

"Sometimes adults don't talk to each other anymore for different reasons," she tried to explain. "Sometimes adults just don't get along, no matter how hard they try. That's what happened with me and your dad, but we both love you very much."

James made an impatient sound and sat up in bed. "I'm not talking about Dad. You need to talk to Harrison, because otherwise Dad will come back, and you'll be sad again."

He said it with such childish conviction that Sara couldn't help but wonder if he were speaking the truth. Harrison would help her fight Kyle in any legal battle. He understood that James was her world, and he'd accepted her son with only patience and love. Her heart hurt thinking about him.

Could she get him back, despite everything that had happened?

James yawned, and Sara gently pushed him back into bed. He didn't protest. Snuggling into his blankets, he fell asleep within moments, although not before mumbling something about going fishing. She smiled. Harrison had promised James that they'd go fishing, hadn't he?

"I love you," she said as she kissed James's forehead. Flicking off his light, she shut his bedroom door.

"You were right," she said as she sat down next to Ruth on the couch. "I have been a coward. I was too scared to be with Harrison because I was afraid of what might happen. That he might turn into another Kyle." Her eyes shone as she looked at her mom. "But Kyle was wrong. I deserve better. He's the one who should be unhappy, not me."

"Oh, Sara. Come here." Ruth enveloped her in a hug, which Sara didn't even realize she needed. "I know you can get him back. That man adores you. He's probably waiting outside in the bushes just to see you walk past."

She snorted a laugh. "You think so?"

"I know so. I'm old enough to know the obvious, my dear. Go get your man and live the life you've more than earned. And if he's stupid enough not to take you back? Well, you already know I have a shotgun at the ready."

Sara just smiled and snuggled against her mom, hopeful for the future for the first time in a while.

19

When Harrison saw that Sara was calling him, his heart leapt into his throat and he almost dropped his phone on the hardwood floor of his bedroom. He swore, rustling around underneath the bed to grab his still ringing phone. He managed to pick it up a second before the call would've gone to voicemail.

"Sara? How are you?" he answered in a rush.

Silence. Then: "Harrison?"

That was definitely not Sara's voice. If he didn't know better, it sounded like a little boy's.

"James?"

"Yeah, it's me. How did you know it was me?"

Harrison sat down on his bed. "Call it a lucky guess. Why are you calling me? Are you okay? Is your mom okay?"

James made a noise. Harrison couldn't tell if it was a grunt, a laugh, or maybe just a six-year-old boy's sound of frustration at stupid adults. "She's fine. She doesn't know I'm using her phone, though. So you can't tell her. She gets mad if I use it without permission."

Harrison was tempted to ask how James knew her passcode, but then again, kids were savvy with technology in this day and age. He probably knew how to use his mother's phone better than she did.

"Okay, I won't tell her, if you tell me why you're calling. You sure you're all right?"

"I'm *fine*. It's my mom. She's sad."

Harrison sat up straighter. "James, has something happened?" His heart raced, and he tried not to think of all of the horrible things that could've happened to Sara. *Car crash, kidnapping, house fire...Oh God, I need to find her right now.*

"She's in the kitchen right now. I'm in my bedroom. You need to talk to her." James said this in a no-nonsense voice that eased some of Harrison's tension.

If something were truly wrong, he wouldn't sound so... annoyed, Harrison thought. His heart calmed somewhat.

"I'd like to talk to her, but she told me she doesn't want to talk to me. Has she changed her mind?"

"She told my grandma she wants to talk to you but she doesn't know how. I think that's dumb, because all you need to do is push your name to call you. Look, I did it, and I'm talking to you. Moms are stupid." James let out a deep sigh.

"Your mom isn't stupid. Being an adult means things can get complicated." Harrison inhaled. "Did your mom really say that to your grandma?" *And am I really getting love advice from a first grader? Talk about desperate.*

"Yeah, I heard her. She's said it, like, a million times now." James paused, and Harrison heard something moving. "I have to go. My mom's coming. You're going to call her, right? Promise me."

"I will. I promise. Now give your mom her phone back."

"Oh, also I wanted to tell you that my grandma has bingo on Wednesday nights—"

The line went dead, but not before Harrison heard Sara's voice asking what James was doing with her phone.

Staring at his phone, he couldn't stop the laugh that bubbled up from his throat.

She wants to talk to me. What the hell do I do now?

He needed a plan. He needed to go straight over there. Wait, James had given him an important tip. Ruth would be gone from the house on Wednesday night.

Harrison smiled. Whoever said kids weren't clever? James would be a complete menace when he was older. Harrison just hoped that Sara didn't look at her recently made calls and put two and two together. Then again, James was probably smart enough to delete his call to Harrison in the first place.

"God save us from too smart kids," he muttered with a laugh.

It was Monday night. Harrison would have forty-eight hours to figure out what the hell he was going to do.

He just prayed it was enough time.

STANDING ON SARA'S DOORSTEP, flowers in hand, Harrison knocked. And waited. His heart pounded like crazy, and when no one answered the door, he almost knocked again.

Then, the door opened.

And there was Sara, looking so beautiful all words vanished.

"Harrison," she whispered. "What are you...?"

He handed her the flowers, a bright blue bouquet of hydrangeas, the same color as her eyes. "Can I come in?" he asked.

She didn't speak, and she didn't take the bouquet either. Oh God, had James lied? Or misunderstood?

Finally, she opened the door to let him in. He stepped inside, handing her the flowers. She took them after a moment's hesitation.

"Thank you. They're beautiful." Her gaze darted around him before she murmured, "Let me get some water for them."

As she rushed to the kitchen, he went to sit in her living room. Clearly, she wasn't remotely excited to see him. Dread filled him, and he struggled to find the words to convince her that they were still meant to be together.

She came back, flowers now in a crystal-clear vase. She set them on the coffee table before sitting down next to him. Stiff and formal, she made sure to place almost a foot of space between them.

Screw arguments. He wasn't going to let her sit there like he was some random cousin she hadn't seen in over a decade. He opened his mouth to speak, but she spoke first.

"I'm sorry." She swallowed. "I'm so sorry, Harrison. I was such an idiot to say those things to you. I think about that night every day, and I regret every word."

"I shouldn't have pushed you so hard," he admitted. "My mom —what she said was unforgivable. I wanted you to know that I've broken with my mom over it. She refused to apologize, and that was the last straw for me."

"You can't." Her eyes widened. "I mean, you can't break up with your *parents*. Not over me. I'll never be your mother's biggest fan, of course, but I couldn't expect you to cut off all contact—"

He shushed her. "I did, and I will. My dad has stood with my mom, but I know he doesn't agree with what she did. The family's struggling, and I hate that." Reaching out, he touched her silken cheek. "But you, Sara Flannigan? You're worth all of that and more. I'd break up with my mother a million times over to be with you. Because I love you."

Her eyes filled with tears, and when she didn't say anything, Harrison wondered if he'd done something wrong. Oh God, did she no longer love him? Had he come here in vain?

"I don't deserve that kind of sacrifice, but thank you. Thank you for loving me, and putting up with me, and not giving up on me." Her tears flowed harder, and then to his delight, she threw her arms around his neck. "I love you so much that I think I might die if you aren't around. Can you ever forgive me?"

His heart soared. "Already forgiven." Pulling back to look into her eyes, he wiped her tears away.

"I realized something this past week. That I pushed you away because I was too scared. You were right, you know. I was being a coward, but I don't care what anyone else thinks of me, or of us being together. Our love will be strong enough to withstand whatever comes."

Harrison gazed down at her, and he couldn't resist the pull: he kissed her. Their lips met, and they kissed each other with all of the hunger that had been building since their separation. He tasted the salt of her tears and the sweetness of her mouth, and he groaned with desire. If he weren't sitting here in her living room with James just down the hallway...

He broke the kiss. "James," he said suddenly.

Sara blinked. "James...? Is in his bedroom...?"

At that, Harrison burst into laughter, but Sara just gave him a confused look. She touched his shoulder, like she was afraid he'd finally lost his mind.

"Your son is a terrifying little boy," he said as he laughed. "He called me to tell me that I should talk to you."

Her eyes widened. "He *called* you? How? Why? When? Good lord, do I want to know what he said to you?"

"He called to tell me that you were sad and wanted to talk to me, but you didn't know what to say."

Sara groaned. "Save me from overly smart six-year-old boys. That was what he was doing with my phone on Monday? I thought he was playing Candy Crush!"

"He also told me that I should wait until Wednesday when your mom was at bingo."

At that, Sara started laughing, too. "He did not? Oh my God! I can't believe this. Getting schooled by a first grader in my own house!"

They laughed together, and it was the first time Harrison felt his heart lighten since everything had happened. They kissed again, and he couldn't stop himself from tipping her over onto the couch, running his hands down her body with a fervency that was only matched by the tangling of their tongues and the touch of their lips.

"Ew, what are you doing? Are you *biting* my mom?"

Harrison sat up to see a disgruntled little boy face looking at him from across the living room. James looked at them both like he'd just seen them eating bugs.

Sara snorted with laughter just as Harrison said, "I was just kissing her. I took your advice, didn't I?"

"I said to *talk* to her, not bite her!"

That just made him and Sara laugh harder, although James glared at them. When they only kept laughing, he shrugged and returned to his room, probably thinking that adults were crazy and could never be fully explained.

"I want to make love with you," Harrison murmured in her ear, "but I'm afraid of getting interrupted again. So I'm just going to imagine it for now."

She smiled. "I'm imagining it, too. When my mom gets back, we can go to your place."

His body heated at the suggestion. He had to restrain himself from counting down the hours until Ruth returned from bingo.

As they waited, they recounted what had happened since their fight. Sara told him about her run-in with Kyle, which made Harrison tense with anger.

"He said that he was going to sue for custody. I'm not sure if it's still just posturing at this point, but there's no way I have the money to fight him in court."

"We'll fight him together, baby. And I'll take him out back and beat him to a pulp if I have to," he vowed as he gazed into her eyes. "I'll never let him take your son from you."

Her eyes filled with grateful tears, and they kissed again.

"Besides, do you think James would willingly go live with his dad? He'd probably make his life hell and he'd pack him up and ship him right back to you," Harrison said with a smile.

"You're probably right. He's too smart of a kid for his own good."

James returned to the living room, and seeing them not kissing —or biting—anymore, he clambered up onto the couch to sit between them. "Harrison, look at this coloring back I just got. It has bugs in it!"

Sara gave him an *I'm sorry* look, but Harrison didn't mind. He'd missed James as much as he'd missed Sara, and he hoped one day that James would consider him a father figure.

"What's your favorite bug again? Ladybug?"

James snorted. "Ladybugs are boring. I like grasshoppers. They can jump four feet into the air."

"Tell Harrison about the praying mantis you found the other day," Sara prompted.

By the time Ruth arrived home, James had dozed off with his head on Harrison's shoulder. When she came into the living room, she gave the trio a look, shook her head, and said, "I'll put him to bed. You two get out of here."

They arrived at Harrison's place in record speed. Sara couldn't stay the night since she had work in the morning, and of course Harrison did as well, but they didn't care. They were finally together again. Harrison opened the passenger side door and reached inside, lifting Sara into his arms. She squealed in surprise.

"Are you taking me over the threshold?"

"That, and you were moving way too slowly. Plus, I can walk faster."

She pinched him for that remark.

He carried her straight to his bedroom, where they stripped each other of their clothes with hurried movements. In between kisses, they took off one garment and the next, laughing when Harrison got stuck in his shirt and when Sara couldn't unhook her bra fast enough. Then they were rolling across the bed, skin to skin, trying to get as close as humanly possible.

Harrison licked at her throat, tasting the salt of her skin, and she arched underneath him. He moved down her torso, feasting on her breasts. She moaned his name when he sucked a nipple into his mouth. He played with her until her nipples were red berries, succulent and irresistible. But he needed to taste all of her —the soft skin at her pelvis, the freckle on her hip, the downy silken skin behind her knee. When he reached her sex, he found her wet with desire, and he parted her with gentle fingers before kissing at the heart of her.

Sara gasped as he licked and swirled his tongue, tasting her, loving the response of her body to his touch. He could feel her limbs quivering, and he had to push her hips down onto the bed to keep her steady. When he pushed a finger and then another inside her, she panted. He could feel that she was close. He suckled her clit as he hooked his fingers inside her, and she came with a loud, seemingly unending moan.

"I love you," she whispered when he moved up her body.

He kissed her, caressing her body, and she took his hardened cock in her hand. He let her stroke him—once, twice, three times —but he couldn't wait any longer. He practically pulsed with the need to be inside her. Flipping them so she sat on top of him, he thrust up against her. His cock pushed through her wet core, which only made them both let out sounds of desperation.

"Take me inside you," he said, gripping her hips.

Sara, with her hair falling down her shoulders and her eyes bright with desire, smiled as she very slowly took him inside her. It was almost painful, being enveloped by her tightness and heat. Inch by inch she took him inside her until he was within her completely. Her hands twitched on his chest, and he watched in satisfaction as a flush crawled up her body in increments.

"God, you're beautiful."

She planted her hands on his chest and, leaning down slightly, began to move. They both closed their eyes as she rode him. Her rhythm was slow and steady, and Harrison had to restrain himself from taking over. He forced himself to open his eyes and watch her, but that only made things worse. With her breasts bouncing, her head tipped back and her eyelashes fluttering, she looked like some kind of goddess come down to haunt his every breath.

Her movements started getting jerky, and when she pushed down on him, he thrust upward. She gasped, her eyes flying open.

"I love you." She dug her fingers into his chest as he began to thrust harder and harder. "I love you so much."

He captured her mouth with his. The sound of their bodies slapping against one another, the creak of the headboard, and their moans and gasps filled the room. Sweat slicked their bodies.

Sara broke their kiss to gasp, "I'm coming. Oh my God!" She screamed, and Harrison shouted a moment later with his own release. He filled her with endless pumps, and as she trembled and shivered around him, he could only dig his fingers into her hips and hold on. Otherwise, he was fairly certain he'd float away from sheer euphoria.

He didn't know many minutes passed before they even moved. They collapsed against the bed, panting and sweaty, and he gathered her into his arms. Laying her head on his shoulder, she smiled up at him. He kissed her forehead.

"I love you," she murmured some time later. "Thank you for waiting for me."

He opened his eyes, and although it was dark, he was sure he could see her eyes shining with the same love that had filled her voice. "I love you, too," he murmured. "I'd wait for you until the end of time."

EPILOGUE

*S*ara smiled as she looked outside her kitchen window. "Look at this grasshopper," Harrison was saying with all the seriousness of a true insect collector, "It's huge."

She watched as James narrowed his eyes. "I've seen bigger," he said in confident tones.

Harrison seemed nonplussed, but with a devious smile, he placed the grasshopper on James's shoulder. James squealed, especially when the grasshopper hopped into his hair. This resulted in Harrison plucking the offending bug from James's hair, but not before both had collapsed to the grass in laughter.

It was the beginning of summer, and with that came three months off for Sara and James. It also meant that Harrison was at their house as often as his schedule permitted. He'd hinted to her about moving in with him, but she didn't want to uproot James after they'd just moved to this house, not to mention that she had Ruth to consider as well.

"They look good together," Ruth commented as she came to stand by the window. "You'd think he was his real dad."

Sara smiled even wider. "They've really taken to each other, haven't they? James deserves a real father in his life." She couldn't stop the tears that threatened, but they were happy tears. She had a tendency to be a bit of a watering pot when it came to her son. Such was the mother's lot in life, she knew.

Harrison found another bug in the grass—Sara thought it was a cicada—and he showed it to James. James yelled in delight, and the two of them watched the cicada crawl in the grass for a while until it flew away in a burst of wings.

Sara had hoped that Harrison would take to James, but she hadn't expected how much he would embrace the role. He'd taken James on that fishing trip he'd promised, and when they returned, sunburned and happy, James had regaled her with the story of their trip for weeks later. He'd been especially fond of the part when they'd had to stick worms on the hooks. "They were so slimy," he'd said with relish. "And they'd still be wiggling even after you poked them with the hook!"

As far as James's real father, Kyle had tried to pursue legal action against Sara in his fruitless pursuit for custody. But the attorney long associated with the Thornton family had been able to block all attempts made by Kyle's lawyer. Kyle, in an angry voicemail, had told Sara that he would leave things alone. For now. She knew that he didn't have a leg to stand on. James would never be given over to Kyle, especially when unsavory aspects regarding some shady financial deals had come to light, thanks once again to Harrison's connections.

"When is he going to pop the question?" Ruth gave her a searching look.

Sara tried not to smile again, but she failed miserably. "It's too early to talk about marriage," she said primly.

Ruth snorted. "You guys were practically going to elope two months ago. Don't tell me he hasn't mentioned it. And really, why not get married if you want to? You can't live apart like this for much longer."

At that, Sara turned toward her mom. "If we get married, what about you? I moved here to help you."

"Which I'm extremely grateful for, but I'll make do."

Sara knew that Ruth couldn't afford this house without her continued financial assistance, but Ruth would never admit it. *I'll ask Harrison what he thinks we should do,* she thought. She filed that away in her mind to bring up tonight.

James yelled, and he and Harrison got up to chase a butterfly with his net. She'd never imagined a lot of things happening in her life, and one of them was watching a six-foot tall physician help her young son chase a butterfly down the street outside her house.

Later that evening, Harrison and Sara stood at the deck of his sailboat, watching the sunset over the lake. With his arms around her waist, Harrison rested his chin on top of her head. They didn't speak, but they didn't need to. Everything about the moment spoke for itself.

The lake shimmered around them, and the sky burst with colors: scarlet and umber and gold, it was like the sky had been painted with jewels. Birds circled overhead, and Sara heard the sound of another boat sailing past them some yards away. If she looked closely, she was sure she could see fish swimming near the surface of the lake.

It was so beautiful that it made her heart ache.

"I've been thinking lately," she said into the silence, her voice quiet. "I think you should talk to your mom."

Harrison groaned. "We've already discussed this."

"I know, but we should discuss it again."

He just tightened his arms around her, silent and still.

She turned to face him. "You can't avoid your parents for the rest of your life, not living in the same town as them. It isn't right. Don't you want to make things right?"

"I feel like you're forgetting what my mother did. To you."

"I'll never forget what she said to me." She shook her head. "She was wrong, but she's tried to reach out and apologize to you, and to me. Shouldn't we take the olive branch when it's offered?"

"It's not that simple, Sara."

"Of course it is. I'm not saying we tell her she wasn't wrong, or that we forget. We don't have to be her biggest fans. I'll probably never really *like* her, but I know what it's like to be estranged from your parent." She swallowed. "I didn't have a relationship with my mom when she was drunk all of the time. Part of me hated her every existence. 'Why couldn't I have a normal mom?' I thought every day. Some days I wished she'd disappear. But now... now I have a chance to have a mom for the first time." She caught his gaze and held it, trying to make him see how important this was. "Your parents won't be around forever, Harrison. Don't let this keep you from them until it's too late."

He didn't say anything, but she watched as his jaw unclenched. Finally, he sighed. "How did you get to be so wise? And forgiving?"

She smiled against his shoulder. "Not wise. Just experienced. Anyway, I'm so happy that I want everyone else to be happy, too."

"Even somebody like Devin Yates?" Harrison asked wryly.

She wrinkled her nose. "Okay, maybe not him. He can rot."

Harrison burst out laughing at that.

To Sara's relief, Devin had been fired from his position at Fair Haven Elementary after getting caught stealing from none other than the raffle for the spring bake sale. As far as anyone knew, he'd hightailed it out of town and hadn't been heard from since. *Good riddance.*

"I love you," Harrison said as they sat down together on a nearby deck chair. "You know that, right?"

"I think so," she teased. "You only tell me three times a day. The days you only say it once I'm usually concerned that you've forgotten about me."

"Brat." He tugged at a strand of her hair with a grin. "How did you get so mouthy? I swear the woman I fell for was always sweet and biddable."

"*Biddable?* What alternate universe have you been living in? And since when have you been reading Jane Austen novels?" She put a hand to his forehead. "I think you have a fever."

"If I do, it's because I'm on fire for you."

She bit her lip. Tried to stop herself. But the laughter came out anyway, and the result was that Harrison tickled her until she cried for mercy.

The moon had risen high in the sky when Harrison kissed Sara's cheek and disentangled himself from her embrace. She made a noise of protest, as she'd been warm and drowsy in his arms, but she came wide awake when he kneeled down in front of her.

Pulling a velvet box from his pocket, he opened it as he said, "Sara Flannigan, the love of my life and the woman of my dreams: will you marry me?"

He didn't even get the words out before she nodded and threw her arms around his neck. Laughing, he kissed her, making sure he didn't drop the ring somewhere it would never be found again.

"Oh my God, yes, yes, yes," Sara was saying. "Of course I'll marry you."

They were sitting on the deck now, all limbs and laughter, and Harrison took the ring box from on top of the chair. Taking the ring out, he cleared his throat. "Put out your hand," he said solemnly.

Just as solemnly, she gave him her left hand. He slowly placed the ring on her finger, and the diamond winked in the moonlight.

"It's beautiful." She held up the ring to see it better. "I love it. I love *you.*"

"I love you, too." He gathered her into his arms again and, after kissing her, added, "I just have one request, though."

She raised her eyebrows.

"James can't have any bugs at the wedding."

"Not even one single solitary grasshopper?"

"Not even one. But when we get back from our honeymoon, I'll take him out to collect as many creepy-crawlies as his heart desires."

She smiled until her heart felt like it would burst. "You have yourself a deal."

~

MEGAN HEARD him before she saw him. She'd know his step anywhere—confident, commanding. *Loud.* How had he gotten to be a police officer, stomping around like that? He'd alert any nearby criminal to his presence just from his boots hitting the ground.

"You open, or did your sign lie to me?"

She turned slowly to face him. Caleb Thornton. The "thorn" in his name was apt, given that he'd been a thorn in her side ever since that night.

And not for the reasons everyone thought.

Megan swallowed and tried to push away her sudden jitters. He always did this to her, and she *hated* it. Why did he have to be so damn handsome and charming? With his dark hair and eyes, and that grin that set a flame inside of her with a mere quirk of his lips? Here he stood in her bakery the Rise and Shine, and to her consternation, they were alone in the store. She'd told his sister Jubilee that she could go home for the afternoon since business had been slow. Now she wished she had Jubilee around as a kind of shield from her too-attractive older brother.

"What do you want?" Megan practically barked. She winced inwardly at her shrewish tone.

"And that's how you treat customers." He clucked his tongue.

Leaning down onto her counter, he drawled, "How do you manage to stay in business?"

She rolled her eyes. "Get off my counter. And I stay in business by serving *people*, not jerks like you."

"A jerk? Madam, you wound me. Straight through the heart." Caleb covered his chest—his very nice, muscular chest, that was covered in his police uniform at the moment.

"You don't have a heart. Now, are you going to order, or are you just going to harass me?"

He seemed to consider the question, but he finally said, "I'd like a cinnamon roll. Please."

"You want that heated up?" She moved to the case to get the cinnamon roll in question.

"I would. Melted frosting is one of my favorite things." He said the words in a low tone that sent shivers down Megan's spine.

I could lick frosting off of him, she thought.

She pushed the thought away. She was not going to give into her attraction to Caleb Thornton. He was a pain in the ass, a jerk, and not worth her time. She practically threw the cinnamon roll in his face, but he only laughed.

Definitely a jerk.

"Anything else?" she asked in a prim voice.

"Actually, there is something." He gazed into her eyes after she'd handed him his receipt, and she forced herself not to look away. "Why do you hate me so much?"

She froze. The moment collapsed into silence, and she wondered what game he was playing. Then, in a tight voice: "If you don't know, you're stupider than I thought."

"Enlighten me, then. Is this really about what happened over ten years ago?"

No, yes, sort of, she wanted to blurt. She looked away and started to walk to the back of the bakery. "If you don't need anything else, I have bread that needs kneading."

She didn't get far. Caleb maneuvered around the counter and, now standing in front of her, took her by the elbow in a firm grip. "You didn't answer my question."

"I don't need to answer your questions. Unless I'm under arrest —again?"

He sighed loudly, and she used that to her advantage to get free of his grip. She walked to the kitchen in the back, but Caleb only followed her.

"Look, I don't know why you're still mad about what happened ten years ago," he said in a frustrated voice. "I was doing my job. What else did you want me to do? You could've gotten yourself hurt."

Megan grabbed the bowl of rising dough and set it down on the counter. She began to knead the dough in earnest, like she could beat into it every feeling she didn't want to feel right this moment.

"I don't want to talk about this right now. Please leave."

He didn't leave, but he didn't keep talking, either. She looked up at him. His expression was...pained. Like she'd hurt him somehow.

She grimaced and searched for her rolling pin. Digging through the sink where a variety of utensils lingered, she found the rolling pin—and subsequently cut the side of her left hand with a knife that she didn't see until it was too late.

"Shit!" She pressed her fingers into her hand, but the bleeding was enough to drip onto the floor at her feet. She swore again, searching for something to bind it with.

"Here." Caleb approached her, rather like you would approach a wounded animal. He didn't touch her until she nodded tightly. Taking her bleeding hand, he turned on the sink and rinsed the wound with lukewarm water. She hissed in pain.

"I'm sorry. That's a wicked cut. I think you might need stitches."

She shook her head. "I'll be fine. I've had plenty of injuries doing this, although"—she hissed again when he pressed a clean towel against the wound before tying it around her hand—"this one is probably one of the worst."

"Hold your hand up," he ordered. "If it stops bleeding here soon, then I won't take you down to the ER."

She did as he said, lifting her injured hand above her heart. To her dismay, he hadn't let her hand go. He held it up with her, and she became too aware of him. Of his height, his heat, his scent. He was almost a head taller than her, and although he was almost on the lanky side, he wasn't remotely skinny or weak. Far from it. She'd seen him take down unruly drunks in bars, and she remembered the hardness of his chest when he'd taken her into his arms.

She closed her eyes. *I can't do this. Not with Caleb Thornton. He ruined everything.*

But her mind didn't seem to want to listen to her heart. Or maybe it was just her libido. She hadn't had sex since she'd broken up with her boyfriend over a year ago, and with Caleb standing so close that she could see the dark stubble on his jaw, she suddenly wished he'd lean down and kiss her. Touch her and God help her, lift her onto the counter and make her forget everything.

Memories flooded her. She pushed them away. She saw in his gaze when he remembered, though, and his eyes darkened. His jaw clenched, and she stifled a gasp when his grip tightened on her hand. Not enough to hurt—never that. Just to let her know that he still held her, and she wouldn't be able to free herself without a struggle.

Why was it that she didn't want to be free from this man?

Her arm was starting to ache from holding it up. She began to lower it, and he finally let go of her. Untying the towel, she saw that the wound had stopped bleeding for the most part. She sighed in relief.

"Looks like you'll be okay," he said in a gruff voice.

She jolted at the sound of his voice. "Yeah, I guess," she said as she retied the towel. "Good thing, considering my insurance is terrible. I really didn't want to pay for an ER visit on top of everything else I have to deal with."

"I'll be right back," he said before he left the kitchen.

Megan blinked. And then he returned with a first-aid kit in his hand. Opening the case, he pulled out antibiotic ointment, gauze, and some bandages. "You'll need to keep the wound clean, otherwise you'll still end up in the ER if you're not careful. That was a pretty deep cut. Here, give me your hand. Let's get you bandaged up. You can't walk around with a towel around your hand."

She didn't know why, but she let him take care of her. After washing his hands and putting on some gloves, he untied the bloodied towel, tossing it into the nearby trashcan. He cleaned the wound, which stung like hell, and he made soothing sounds in the back of his throat when she wanted to cry out from the pain. His fingers were infinitely gentle as he wrapped her hand with the gauze before taping it closed. And then he touched the back of her hand—so quickly, that she wondered if she'd imagined it.

"There." His voice was gruff. "Keep it clean, and you should be okay. I'd probably change the bandage tonight."

She cradled her hand to her chest. "Thank you."

"You're welcome."

They stared at each other, so many words unspoken. Megan wished they were anybody else in the entire world. Then maybe this wouldn't be so difficult. And so futile.

Then: "You never did answer my question," he said.

She raised her eyebrows. "Which one was that?"

"Why you hate me so much." But he said it with that heart-stopping grin.

The previous moment shattered, for which she was both thankful and disappointed. Rolling her eyes, she pointed to the exit. "Go eat your cinnamon roll and leave me alone already, Caleb Thornton."

He tipped his hat. "Yes, ma'am. But one day, I'll get you to answer my question."

She just smiled to herself as she watched him—and his tight backside—leave her kitchen.

WANT MORE OF THE THORNTONS?

Don't miss out on the next in the series!

THE VERY THOUGHT OF YOU
(Caleb and Megan's story)

Turn the page for an exclusive excerpt!

"I hope you like sushi," Caleb said after he and Megan were seated at a booth in the corner, "because otherwise tonight won't be much fun for you."

Megan wrinkled her nose. "Lucky for you that I do like sushi. Although what would've happened if I'd said I hated it? Would you go somewhere else with me?"

He heaved a deep sigh. "I guess. Although I would've judged you for it for the entire evening."

Laughing, Megan felt her nerves calm for the first time that evening. Ever since Caleb had come into The Rise and Shine and insisted that she go to dinner with him, she'd been a mess. Actually, she'd been a mess over him for what felt like an eternity. Now that she was sitting across from him, his dark hair tousled and his face showing the shadow of his beard already, she had to stop herself from practically crawling into his lap and eating him up. It didn't help that he was wearing a button-up that brought out the green in his eyes, or that he looked at her like he could eat her up, too, if given half the chance.

Megan drank almost her entire glass of water before they'd even ordered.

"What are you getting?" Caleb asked as he set down his menu.

"The sashimi platter. And no, I'm not sharing, although I do appreciate that you'll be paying for it."

He tipped his head back and laughed, and she drank in the lines of his throat as he laughed. *He's way too handsome,* she thought petulantly. If only he had a receding hairline, or a paunch, or overly long nose hair. Something to temper his handsomeness and make him less intimidating in that regard. It didn't help that their waitress eyed him with obvious interest, or that other women in the restaurant had almost fallen out of their chairs when he'd walked in.

Megan scowled. She didn't have time to deal with a man as handsome as Caleb Thornton. Didn't she know going out with him would be bad news?

When Caleb gave her a glance that sent her body aflame, she cleared her throat and asked, "Any news about my favorite criminal?"

Caleb frowned. "Nothing yet. It's like this guy is a fucking ghost. We did have a tip today that I hope will give us something more substantial to investigate."

Megan's ears perked up. "Really?"

"I shouldn't tell you this, but I'm not on duty right now. This same guy was spotted at Clover Park yesterday evening. A woman was jogging and noticed he was following her."

"Is she all right?"

He nodded. "She arrived home before he could do anything, but he also didn't wear a mask over his face this time. She was able to identify that he has a scar on his lower lip about three inches long. That's not exactly something you see on a lot of people, so it helps us for obvious reasons."

Megan sat back in her booth, considering. Once they caught this guy, Caleb wouldn't be around her bakery anymore, would he? Their association would end, and she couldn't stop her throat from closing at the thought. It was stupid, but she didn't want it to end. Caleb drove her crazy. She wanted to strangle him almost as often as she wanted to kiss him. And yet...through all of this, he'd been her one constant.

She smiled wanly. "I'm glad you got something legitimate. I'm tired of looking over my shoulder, afraid that he's found me and is going to do whatever it is he thinks he wants to do."

"I won't let that happen," he vowed. "He won't put a finger on you—not on my watch."

"I know."

Their entrees soon arrived, and the evening was taken up with eating and enjoying each other. Megan playfully slapped his hand away when he tried to snag some of her sashimi, while she stole multiple pieces of tempura when he wasn't looking. He told her he'd get his revenge for that, which only made her shiver with delight.

She also noticed that Caleb didn't order any alcohol. She wondered if her admission that she didn't drink anymore had affected him somehow, or at the very least, he didn't drink out of consideration for her. Her heart swelled.

When she sipped her water, the bite of wasabi hot on her tongue, he pointed his chin at her choice of beverage.

"So you don't drink at all?"

She stilled. Her fingers curling about the cold glass, she struggled to answer. Why was he asking this now? She didn't want to talk about the past. She never wanted to talk about the past because some things were better off left dead and buried, the bones disintegrating into the earth.

"No, I don't. I haven't since that night." She looked away, refusing to see the pity on his face. His own regrets about that night, when she'd thrown herself at him and he'd pushed her away. Her gut churned and her face heated with embarrassment, even after so many years.

"You were just a dumb kid, you know. Anyone could've gotten screwed up like that. If I had a dollar for how many dumb kids I've arrested for things like that—"

"Don't, Caleb. Please don't." She pushed her food away, no longer hungry. "I really don't want to talk about this."

"Because we've never talked about it. I know you were angry with me for a long time. Are you still angry?"

Her honest answer? She didn't know. Her anger was jumbled up with so many other emotions regarding Caleb that it was difficult to figure out where one thread started and another ended. She'd hated Caleb for many years—for arresting her, for rejecting her. For humiliating her. For indirectly causing her to lose her scholarship and forcing her to stay in Fair Haven when she'd gotten so close to leaving.

"I don't know," she said finally. "It's all so messed up. I wanted to hate you for all eternity. It was easier than confronting what I'd done to screw up my own life."

His eyes darkened, and a well of sadness she'd only glimpsed before shimmered in his eyes. "I get it. I do. You're not the only one who's fucked up." He pushed his fingers through his hair. "Honestly, if anyone were to win that battle, it would be me."

She frowned in confusion. As far as she knew, Caleb Thornton had been a model citizen since he'd been born. He'd gotten good grades, had played sports, had graduated with honors and attended college before returning home to become a police officer. He'd worked his way up in the ranks with determination and sheer hard work.

The look on his face prompted her to say more than she would have otherwise. Perhaps it was the hint of vulnerability in his expression, or her desire to discover what he'd done that still haunted him. Maybe if she opened up, he would as well.

"I think I hated you the most when you told me I was a child when I tried to kiss you." His eyes widened at that, but she just shook her head. "I wanted to seem like an adult, but you destroyed that. You reminded me that I didn't know a damn thing—especially when it came to men."

"Megan, you know good and well that even if I'd wanted you then, I couldn't have acted on it. You were all of seventeen."

"I was going to be eighteen in a month, and you aren't that much older than me. Don't act like you wanted me then. I know your feelings have changed—I think they have—but back then—"

He gritted his teeth. "Do you really think that I don't want you *now*?"

"Considering the hot-and-cold act you like to play, yes." His tone sparked anger deep inside her, and she rather wished they would start fighting again. She could understand fighting with Caleb Thornton. It was the softer moments—the vulnerable moments—where she lost her footing.

"Considering how I kissed you that night in your apartment, and at your bakery today, I think it's fairly clear that I want you."

"Because I'm a challenge. Because I pushed you away the last time we kissed, and you wanted to prove to yourself that you can conquer me. I can just be another notch on your bedpost."

She didn't know where these words were coming from, yet they fell from her mouth like a torrent. Perhaps they'd been buried deep inside her all along, just waiting to be freed. Her doubts clawed at her soul, drawing blood. *Why would he want me now when he'd never really wanted me before?*

And perhaps the greatest question of all: *Who would really want me when no one ever had before?*

They stared at each other, at a stalemate. Caleb seemed incredulous, while Megan wanted to shake him until his teeth rattled.

"If you really think that, then you're not as intelligent as I thought you were."

She stood up and grabbed her purse. "Go to hell, Caleb. I don't have time for this and I don't have time for your bullshit, either."

Stalking out of the restaurant, Megan didn't know where she would go. Caleb had picked her up, and it was too far to walk home. And she wasn't particularly in the mood to walk home at night when the last time she'd done just that, she'd been followed and almost accosted by some creep.

She rubbed her arms as shivers wracked her frame. It wasn't cold outside, but she felt cold. Numb. She gritted her teeth to keep them from chattering.

"Megan! Megan, dammit, wait!" Caleb grabbed her by the

elbow. She pulled away. "What the hell was that all about?" he demanded.

"Just leave me alone. Please. I want to go home. I can't keep doing this with you. All we ever do is fight." She sounded pathetic, desperate, and she was completely exhausted. And above all else, she hated herself for starting this fight in the first place, because it was easier to fight with Caleb than love him.

Her chills only increased with that admission. *I can't love him,* she thought, but she knew it was pointless.

She'd fallen in love with him ages ago before she'd even realized it. Now she was too far in to stop it.

Caleb put his hands on her shoulders as he turned her to face him. "What are we doing, Megan? What is this? Is this really about how I don't want you?"

He wrapped her in his arms, and she could only surrender. His body was hard, and he practically shook with anger. Or maybe it was sheer lust. Megan couldn't know anymore.

"You're an idiot if you think I feel anything for you but complete obsession. You've driven me crazy ever since you tried to kiss me that night when I arrested you. I've wanted you for years, but I told myself you needed a better man than me."

He seemed to struggle for words. "But now? I don't care. I don't care about all of the times I said I'd stay away from you." He gripped her so tightly she could barely breathe. "You're mine, Megan Flannigan, and I don't give a flying fuck if that pisses you off."

He kissed her ruthlessly, and she could only hang onto him. Digging her nails into his shoulders, she opened her mouth to him. He stroked inside her mouth like she knew he would stroke inside her body. She didn't care that they were standing in the middle of the restaurant's parking lot, or that anyone could see them under the streetlamp. She didn't care about anything but being held in Caleb's arms.

ALSO BY IRIS MORLAND

The Thorntons

THE NEARNESS OF YOU

THE VERY THOUGHT OF YOU

IF I CAN'T HAVE YOU

DREAM A LITTLE DREAM OF ME

SOMEONE TO WATCH OVER ME

TILL THERE WAS YOU

Heron's Landing

SEDUCE ME SWEETLY

TEMPT ME TENDERLY

DESIRE ME DEARLY

ADORE ME ARDENTLY

ABOUT THE AUTHOR

A coffee addict and cat lover, Iris Morland writes sexy and funny contemporary romances. If she's not reading or writing, she enjoys binging on Netflix shows and cooking something delicious.

irismorland.com
info@irismorland.com

CPSIA information can be obtained
at www.ICGtesting.com
Printed in the USA
LVOW13s1304210917
549557LV00019B/306/P